Other books by the author:

Playing Out the String, novel
Prosperity, novel

WOMEN IN CARS

B. J. LEGGETT

LIVINGSTON PRESS

THE UNIVERSITY OF
WEST ALABAMA

Copyright © 2018 B. J. Leggett
All rights reserved, including electronic text
ISBN 13: 978-1-60489-204-8 trade paper
ISBN 13: 978-1-60489-205-5 hardcover
Library of Congress Control Number: 2018936405
ISBN: 1-60489-204-8 trade paper
ISBN: 1-60489-205-6 hardcover
Printed on acid-free paper
Printed in the United States of America by
Publishers Graphics

Hardcover binding by HF Group
Typesetting and page layout: Sarah Coffey
Proofreading: Erin Watt, Tricia Taylor, Joe Taylor
Cover layout & photo Jill Knight

first edition
6 5 4 3 3 2 1

WOMEN IN CARS

We are talking now of summer evenings in Knoxville, Tennessee in the time that I lived there so successfully disguised to myself as a child.

—James Agee, *Knoxville: Summer 1915*

In the Knoxville, Tennessee, of this story, the characters, incidents, and institutions are fictitious. Some of the place names are real, but I have rearranged them freely.

PROLOGUE
THE SMELL

On Friday evening the smell has not yet reached its rumored proportions, but the custodian Arthur Inman detects it as he steps off the elevator pushing a canvas bag. He can't place it but knows he has come upon it before, and it hangs at the edge of his memory like a scene from childhood. Later he will say that he recognized it the second it hit him, and that will add to his difficulties, as the transcript of his interrogation confirms.

Q: If you knew what it was, then why didn't you go into the Head's office?

A: He told me not to clean his office.

Q. But the smell . . .

A. He was real definite.

Q. [Expletive.] Does that make any sense to you? Middle of the night? Nobody around?

A. He said not to go in his office.

In fact, it is only as he is leaving the third floor to continue his rounds that it comes to him.

Inman, it is later reported, has spent the past several hours in a bar called Kelly's waiting for his shift to begin. He will, in the course of the investigation, be characterized as "unbalanced" by Sergeant Foulkes, his interrogator, and "barely functional," by Charles Durrell, Associate Professor of English, whose office he cleans, but whatever his mental state, his immediate problem is that he has consumed a considerable amount of alcohol, as his bar tab, produced by Kelly himself, makes clear.

Inside the English Office, he flips on the lights and notes that the smell is stronger—surprising since three is his easiest floor, administrators and secretaries. Four is a different matter. Some of the people on four eat lunch in their offices and throw pieces of half-eaten God-knows-what in the trash. But this is not the smell of garbage, he reckons, then loses his train of thought, distracted momentarily by a long-buried scene—his grandfather's farm in Lenoir City, the slaughterhouse, the smell of wood smoke and the other smell.

The odor and the memory stay with him as he makes his way among the three desks in the office, emptying the waste paper into the canvas bag. At the middle desk he stoops to look at a framed photograph, a couple and a child on a beach. He studies the young mother in the tiny bathing suit, then straightens, pushes the canvas bag to the last desk and pauses before the door that leads into the adjoining room. The metal plate identifies the office of J. Hollis Sanders, Head, Department of English. He feels something sticky under his foot and bends down to wipe it up with the towel he keeps tucked under his belt. Another surprise for three. Wouldn't surprise him on four at all. Turning to leave, he notices a smudge by the light switch and gives it a swipe with the towel, turns off the lights, and shuts the door behind him.

He pushes the canvas bag down the lighted hallway, obsessed now with the smell. As he enters the elevator it comes into focus in his head—the smells of the slaughterhouse, the carcass hanging from the metal hook. And he is taken back to the farm in Lenoir City in the early winter when he was first permitted to witness the annual ritual of hog killing.

*

By Monday morning the character of the smell has changed. It is now a stench. Margaret Bains, Head Secretary and Office Supervisor, enters at 7:30 and presses a hand to her mouth. She casts about for the source, walks hesitantly through the outer office and enters the smaller office of J. Hollis Sanders. The scene spread before her will in numerous versions, some of them demonstrably exaggerated, make its way around campus for the remainder of the spring semester. She does not take it in at once, but as her eyes sweep the room she begins to moan softly. Dutiful head secretary to the end, she recovers her senses long enough to telephone the campus police before vomiting directly into the out-tray on her desk.

In the preface to his semi-autobiographical novel based loosely on the J. Hollis Sanders affair, Charles Durrell writes: "Next to defecation, vomiting is the single most repulsive bodily function. The disgorging of the contents of the stomach through the mouth is so repugnant to us that we wish to put it out of mind as quickly as possible. So it is easy to see why the campus police should have missed the significance of the secretary's violation of her out-tray—at least until it was too late. Had she chosen a more romantic reaction to what she had just witnessed—fainting perhaps—or had she chosen a different target for her emission, events would almost certainly have taken a different turn. On the other hand, it would have been a much less engaging affair, not, in any event, one worthy of being fictionalized."

MONDAY

CHAPTER ONE
THE WOMEN IN CARS MYSTERY

The smell of cut grass is pungent enough to call up earlier summers, and Robert Cory stops on the front steps of the Walter Stevens Library to watch a man mowing the lawn in front of the Law College. Waiting for his sight to adjust to the late afternoon light, he piles his books on the steps and sits down to watch the steady motion of the mower, winding down in smaller and smaller squares. He feels groggy and a little disoriented, the way he used to feel as a kid after a Saturday matinee, walking out of the theater into an afternoon so brightly tinted that it seemed less real than the black and white world of the Bijou.

He squints into the low sun and tries to reconstruct the conversation he has just overheard. It had taken him some time to realize that the elderly librarian he saw five days a week was not describing the plot of a novel but a real even—something incredible. He had picked it up in fragments, but it appeared that a man had been killed in his office, an important man, a dean perhaps. His body had been discovered only hours earlier after lying there for days over the spring break. The smell must have been atrocious, the librarian had guessed, wrinkling her nose, then pushed his books across to him with a little smile and turned back to her companion behind the desk.

A dean. Who would kill a dean?

The mower has obliterated the middle patch of his square and Cory rouses himself from the steps and walks to the parking lot behind the Law College. He stows his books in the back seat of a BMW and eases out of the lot into the Jefferson Avenue traffic. He glances at his watch—5:20. He might have made his exit earlier and missed the worst of the rush hour, but he doesn't mind the slow drive. His ex-wife once remarked that he must surely be the one man alive who actually enjoyed being stuck in traffic. The observation is not altogether true, but it captures something essential about him.

He makes his way through the business section west of the university and ponders the dead dean. Who would kill a dean? Another dean perhaps, a rival dean of another college. An associate dean on the way up. But surely in the hierarchy of the university a dean can be eliminated by nothing less than a provost.

Then perhaps he was not killed as a dean but simply as a man. Perhaps he had been discovered in an affair with his secretary or a student or an associate dean. Or perhaps he himself had discovered something . . .

Cory catches himself in mid-thought and grimaces as he brakes in the congestion by Kelly's Bar. He realizes that he is on the brink of a fallacy he has himself described and labeled. It is part of a theory he once called the Women in Cars Mystery, and its essential assumption is that life is not extraordinary but ordinary. What fascinates us, the theory assumes, is the imagination's play in the absence of fact, the mind filling in the blanks—the runaway bride, the disappearance of the pregnant wife. It follows then that only a charming illusion could concoct rich and fascinating mysteries from the death of a dean.

He also remembers quite distinctly the origin of the theory. It had been on a summer evening in Knoxville, Tennessee, in the time that he lived there so successfully disguised as the husband of Sally Cory, an evening much like this one with the same summer smell of cut grass. Jack and Janice Abbott had stopped in for a drink after a movie at the old State Theater on Gay Street where the Federal Office Building now stands. Jack Abbott was in his first year in the English Department at Western Appalachian, and the two couples were in the first year of a blossoming friendship.

It was during the time he and Sally were living in the Sequoyah

Apartments and he was managing the local branch of his father's furniture stores. A time of significant glances and private jokes. But he had not known until later what a good time it was because he was bored with his job and Sally hated the apartment and was even then conducting a campaign to borrow the money from his father for a house she had found on Cherokee Boulevard. An advance on his inheritance, she argued. He remembers her once dancing through the apartment singing, "We're gonna be rich, we're gonna be rich." But that's another story.

This one begins after a drink in the living room of the Sequoyah apartment with Jack Abbott's observation that lately he has been seeing an unusually large number of very attractive women driving alone in expensive cars. "Is there something here I'm missing?" He shakes a cigarette out of the pack, and Cory, sitting in the traffic on Jefferson Avenue, is startled to remember how recently people smoked cigarettes inside their houses.

"I have a theory about that," Cory says, half seating himself on the arm of the sofa beside Janice.

"Why are we not surprised?" Sally is freshening her drink—too soon, he thinks—at the counter that divides the tiny kitchen from the living room.

"Let the man talk," Jack Abbott says. "Why is there never an ashtray in this place?"

"Just use the vase," Sally says. "It's a filthy habit. You should give it up."

"Tell us your theory, Robert." Janice Abbott has a lovely throaty voice. She stretches back on the sofa and smiles up at Cory.

"I've always thought of it as the Brief Encounter or Face in the Crowd theory, but we could just as easily call it the Women in Cars Mystery," Cory says. "It involves the inconsistency Jack has just observed. The number of beautiful women one sees only for a brief moment—in automobiles, for example—is way out of proportion to the number of beautiful women one actually sees routinely, present company excepted of course."

Janice raises her glass to him. "Is there a certain type you have in mind?"

"That's the wonderful part of it. They're beautiful in every conceivable way. You have your tan society types in Mercedes. Secretaries fixing their lipstick in the rear view mirror. Country girls in beat-up old—"

"Oh, please." Sally glares at him from the counter. "Do we have to listen to your sexual fantasies? What about men in cars? Does your theory apply to men?"

"My theory applies to women. You'll have to formulate your own theory about men in cars. I'm sure the same principles apply, but I'm not alone in this. Jack was obviously struck by it too."

"Don't forget the sunglasses," Jack says. "Sunglasses add a touch of mystery."

"I've thought of that, and the fact that their bodies are mostly hidden, but these don't go to the heart of the mystery. Why is the proportion of beautiful women in cars so high?"

"Do you have a solution?" Sally asks.

"There are several solutions, and I'm afraid the one I'm forced to is a little disappointing. It's not nearly as interesting as the problem."

"We were afraid of that." Sally moves to the sofa beside Janice.

"But then that's what recommends it as the true solution. It's so commonplace. It involves a notion you've never accepted." He pauses. "Our illusions about life are always more interesting than the lives we lead, which are, after all, very ordinary. We have glimpses of people as they pass us by, and we imagine that their lives are full of romance and beauty, but if we talked to them for fifteen minutes we would see that they are as dull as everything and everyone else we know."

"Present company excepted of course," Janice says.

Cory raises his glass to her and smiles. "Women in cars are fantasy women, but it's a fantasy we all carry around with us. Our illusion that life is really wonderful after all. It's directly related to the false expectations that make us disappointed with our lot." He waves his glass in a circle to take in the apartment. "It's what makes us think that a house on Cherokee Boulevard would solve everything and make us happy ever after."

Sally gives him an unamused smile. "I don't see what cars have to do with it."

"It doesn't have to be cars. Jack brought up the cars. It could be the Women in Expensive Restaurants Mystery or Women in Glossy Magazine Ads, but they don't have the same ring."

"Women in Kroger," Janice says.

"No, no. That has the opposite effect."

"Women in Walgreens," Jack says.

"Women in Shoe Stores." Janice again, nudging Sally beside her on the sofa.

"Now you're making it absurd."

Well it is absurd, somebody says, and the talk turns to the movie they've just seen and debates whether Woody Allen can really be taken seriously as a lover and then moves to the price of gasoline.

Cory brakes for a gang of skateboarders at the entrance to Tyson Park, the memory trailing off. Or maybe more invention than memory, since he is never quite sure how much was actually said that summer evening and how much his imagination has filled in.

But no matter—no one left to verify or dispute. The little gang that had seemed so solid is scattered now. Sally lives in a condominium in Fox Den and the Abbotts have drinks with other more interesting couples and he spends his time working on a hopelessly complicated book in the university library, avoiding the people who now compose his fantasies.

He has seen Sally only half a dozen times in the years since the divorce, although he occasionally receives second-hand reports of her career as fashion model and dinner-theater actress. He has managed to avoid Jack and Janice altogether.

He has managed to avoid almost everybody altogether. The money allows him to do that. People with money are expected to be a little eccentric, to spend their days in idle solitude. There are always stories about people who suddenly come into a great deal of money, and Cory has heard enough to guess at the kind he has inspired. In keeping with his theory, they are of course much more interesting than the actual circumstances. Essentially, they are stories of the only son of a fine old Knoxville family who, preferring the world of letters, rejects his position as heir to the family business and is cut out of the father's will, replaced by a favorite nephew from North Carolina. They center, however, on the irony of the lovely ambitious wife who, learning of her husband's bleak prospects, divorces him only to discover that the old man has had a death-bed change of heart. Only months after the decree her ex-husband is the possessor of a chain of furniture stores, assorted real estate, and several million dollars.

There are doubtless also stories of attempted reconciliations and rejections and of the husband's eccentric behavior, most specifically his sudden obsession with privacy—"The Hermit," he once overheard in a loud aside. Altogether, it's not a great story, as such things go, but it does have some of the ingredients that feed the imagination—money, love, betrayal, and a beautiful woman.

Given the opportunity, Cory could have corrected a number of the rumors. For one thing, the extent of his wealth has been somewhat exaggerated. It is true he no longer has to work for a living, but his income is not much larger than that of a successful lawyer or physician, and the house on Cherokee Boulevard, the one that Sally always fancied, is a rare indulgence. One of the companies he inherited, a regional chain that rented portable toilets for construction sites, Cory found somehow unseemly and sold almost immediately, using a portion of the proceeds to purchase the house on Cherokee. A few years later, after experiencing the tedium of the world of buying and selling, he sold the furniture stores and then, one by one, the other properties until he was left with the clean slate that is now his life.

As for the ill-timed divorce by the wife, the irony most crucial for making it a good story, that is totally mistaken. Cory's version is simpler and it does not involve the issue of the inheritance.

Returning home a day earlier than expected from a buying trip to North Carolina, so it goes, he had pulled into the apartment parking lot beside a black Mercedes. Inside he saw his wife nestled comfortably against a man he did not recognize but whose face he thought he would never forget.

But that, it turns out, had been a highly romantic reaction. Sitting now at the light of the Neyland-Kingston Pike intersection across from the Unitarian Church, Cory tries to conjure up that face but draws a blank.

Instead he imagines a scene in which a distinguished looking old gentleman lies on a carpet in a pool of blood, a knife, cartoon-like, protruding from his chest. But the murdered dean has ceased to interest him, and the image fades as, waiting for the light to change, he studies the remarkably bland architecture of the Unitarian Church. He would have found it ironic to learn that at this moment, even as his interest dims, events are conspiring to make the dead man (who was not, he will learn, a dean) his sole occupation for the week ahead.

Cory, who is interested in irony, recognizes however that almost any event seen in retrospect takes on an ironic quality. Somewhere in the back seat of the BMW under a *New York Times* piece on the evolutionary function of the female orgasm is a novel titled *Prosperity* by a man named Robert O'Brian, who writes, "If any event is ultimately ironic when seen from the broadest perspective, then the notion of irony loses its distinctive appeal. Irony, in one sense, is only the ignorance of the meaning of the present."

CHAPTER TWO
THE CHANCELLOR'S PLAN

On a first meeting, Michael Joseph O'Connor might seem a poor fit for the position of Chancellor of a large regional university. He comes off as a bit young and brash, bearing little trace of the thoughtful scholarly demeanor assumed to be requisite for the position. Appearances are, however, deceiving and O'Connor has received generally high marks for his five years as Chancellor of Western Appalachian. The faculty respect him because he is indeed a scholar, an historian who maintains the instincts of a professor. The administrators and bureaucrats who viewed his candidacy with some foreboding were relieved to discover that he is a talented executive, decisive and surprisingly tactful when it serves his purposes. His reputation in Stockton Tower, the seat of campus administration, is that of a man who gets things done, keeps his faculty and the legislature happy, and maintains a cool head in a crisis.

Late on Monday afternoon, long after the departure of the secretarial staff, O'Connor is engaged in his current crisis, although his manner betrays no hint of it. Leaning back in a leather chair with his feet on the desk, he taps a pencil idly on a sheet of paper in his lap and stares absently at the two men across the desk. The sheet contains a single column of names, all but three of which have been marked through.

The two men across the desk contemplate identical lists. James Houghton, Assistant to the Chancellor, is a young zoologist assumed to be looking toward a bright future as an administrator. The older man, Edgar Ammons, has been for many years Vice-Chancellor for Academic Affairs. It was he, the heir apparent, who was passed over when O'Connor jumped several positions to become Chancellor.

"I think Robert Cory's our man." O'Connor maintains his nearly horizontal position and awaits a response.

Houghton and Ammons study their sheets, neither betraying the fact that Cory's name has been crossed out on his sheet.

"How did he get on the list?" Ammons asks.

"I believe I suggested him," O'Connor says.

"Everybody else is either faculty or administration," Ammons says. "He's the only outsider."

"He's on the Development Council, and he's given us a lot of money. Do you have a name?"

Houghton watches the two with some interest. He has resolved to try to avoid being drawn into what he regards as an ill-conceived venture.

"I could go with Gerald Rice," Ammons says. "He's a good committee man, gets things done."

"Rice would be a disaster. Can't keep his mouth shut. Anybody else?"

"My second choice would be Charles Travis."

"Travis is in your office. We might just as well do it ourselves."

"He would do a good job."

"I'm not worried about that. If it works out, anybody can look good. I'm thinking about how it's going to look if it doesn't work. Cory's not in the university. He's a friend of the mayor, or at least he used to be—I don't think he's on close terms with anybody now. Which is another point in his favor—it's not going to get spread all over town." O'Connor seems unaware of having switched arguments in mid-sentence. "He's independent, a solid citizen, fine old Knoxville family, country club connections, all that. And he would certainly be acceptable to Deathridge. And to the faculty if we decide to go public. Some of the people in English probably know his work."

"Isn't he thought of as something of an, I don't know, a local character, an eccentric?"

"There are stories. He was divorced from one of the most beautiful women in town just before he got rich—very bad timing on her part. And he seems to prefer his own company to that of anybody else. Something of a hermit. Spends most of his time in our library actually. People can't understand why a man with all that money would rather read books than fuck Sally Cory. Though I must say if you've ever seen her you might wonder about it yourself."

Houghton observes the slightest flinch from Ammons, who has never adjusted to the Chancellor's language.

"I was just wondering about his fitness for the job," Ammons says finally in a tone that signifies his acquiescence.

"If you're implying that he's some kind of fool, you're mistaken. I talked to him at some length at the board meeting last week—really a very charming man."

"Well, if you're determined to go with him," Ammons says.

"No, I want a consensus on this. I've got Robert Cory and two other names on my list."

As O'Connor reads the names, Houghton turns toward the window to hide any semblance of a smile, aware that they are anathema to the Vice-Chancellor.

"If I'm forced to choose from those three, I'll take Cory."

"Okay, Cory's your choice. Jim?"

"Cory's fine with me." Houghton enters the conversation for the first time. "Though why he would let himself get involved in this business is more than I can understand."

"Let me worry about that. Not everybody's conditioned by your extreme caution." With a sweeping gesture of the right hand O'Connor indicates that the conference is over. "I think we've made the right choice. I'll let you know something tomorrow."

In the hallway, Ammons suggests to Houghton that they've made no choice at all, and their work in compiling the list has been a charade. "He had his mind made up from the minute we walked in the room." The Chancellor, he says in a tone of high-principled indignation, is making a bad situation worse. "He'll have a lot of explaining to do if things turn ugly, as I suspect they will. We're looking at a potential Penn State."

"I wouldn't go that far," Houghton says. "Nothing illegal."

"Cover-up."

"That's not quite the right term for what he's trying to do. Maybe damage control. But I have to agree it's risky. I probably should have said something." Houghton stops in the hallway. "At least let him know how I feel." He turns back toward the Chancellor's office. The Penn State reference has set off an alarm.

"Not that it'll do any good," Ammons says. "This is vintage O'Connor. But you tell him what you want to—I'm going home."

When Houghton leans in the doorway he sees that the Chancellor has not moved. He sits with his feet on the desk tapping the pencil on the paper in his lap, a vacant look in his eyes. "I hope you're right in playing it this way," Houghton says. "You could get burned if somebody gets the idea that you're trying to hide something."

"*We* could get burned. Right. I don't have a lot of choice— we've got to keep a lid on it. It couldn't have happened at a worse time—the legislature's in session, budget hearings won't be over for almost a month. They're already up in arms about this Sex Week business. A thing like this, if it turns out to be a real scandal, is all they need to justify whatever they want to do."

"Those people are crazy."

"Exactly. That's why we've got to head 'em off."

"They can hardly blame us for a mur—a death."

"When you're in this business a little longer you'll know that it's not what really happens that matters but how it looks when it gets printed in the morning paper. I don't know why the man was killed, but I've got a great imagination, and I've heard the rumors from time to time. It's the possibility of some juicy little scandal over there that scares the hell out of me. I'm going to keep as tight a rein on it as long as I possibly can."

"This is not *Trent's Last Case* we're talking about, Michael. This is the real world and the man is dead. It's not possible to deal just with the way things look. You can't appoint a committee and hope it'll all go away."

O'Connor is not sure what *Trent's Last Case* is, but he understands Houghton's implication. "Don't tell me about the real world. Sometimes I think I'm the only person in this university who deals with the real world. Aren't you the one who spends his time looking at smears on a glass slide? Christ, I don't need a lecture on the real world."

"All I'm saying is that we're trying to manipulate an event, something that really happened. There's no way to cover it up, and people are going to find it extremely interesting."

"There's nothing more uninteresting than a dead man. What's interesting is how he got to be dead. The only thing I'm trying to do here is keep the story as uninteresting as possible."

"I understand what you're after. You want some control over what gets out."

"As long as we go about our work in a dull way people leave us alone. When we make the papers we got trouble. The Sex Week thing—hell, that was relatively innocent, just some kids trying to put out information in a provocative way. But there was that word like a red flag." O'Connor forms an imaginary headline with his thumb and forefinger. "' Senate Committee Investigates Use of State Funds for Sex Lectures.' They played it for all it was worth, and think about the possibilities here." He forms another headline. "'University Love Triangle Blamed in Department Head's Murder.' I don't know, use your own imagination. It opens us up to the kind of attention we don't need"

"I understand."

"We can't cover it up, but we're sure as hell going to give them as little as possible until the legislature adjourns. Then they can screw themselves for all I care. People have short memories."

"Cory's your way of getting this whole thing out of the Chancellor's office. I understand that. *He'll* be the one on the six o' clock news."

"I hope nobody's on the six o'clock news, but questions are

going to be raised about what's going on over there, and we're going to have to look into it. Why is it that you and Ammons instantly jump to the conclusion that I'm engaged in some sort of Byzantine intrigue? I want an independent person to head the university's part of the investigation, not one of us. That's all—nothing sinister about that." He looks out over the river that provides the view from the choice offices in Stockton Tower. "I'm just trying to run this place so we can do our work."

"Well, at least Edgar's getting some pleasure out of it. He thinks you're digging yourself a hole."

The Chancellor waves his hand dismissively. "He's harmless. Would that all my enemies were as ineffectual as Edgar Ammons."

"Let me know what I can do."

Houghton drops his crumpled list into the wastebasket by the desk. At the door he hears O'Connor saying to no one in particular, "It's exactly like that bastard Sanders to take us all down with him. I should have gotten him out of there a long time ago."

CHAPTER THREE
THE CHANCELLOR'S CALL

The house stands on a bluff looking out over the Tennessee River. It has been angled toward the west, out of line with the other houses on Cherokee Boulevard so that even in winter the afternoon sun floods the front rooms. It afforded, the realtor had said, the finest river view to be had in Sequoyah Hills. Cory, however, spends most of his time in the study, the only dark room of the house. It's a room of books—not a library in the conventional sense, but a stew of things thrown together seemingly at random, paperbacks and heavy hardbound volumes, scholarly journals and popular magazines. They line the four walls and overflow from the shelves to the tables and the floor. A fastidious visitor—he has never entertained one—might have called it a clutter, but there is a loose order to the arrangement that Cory knows so instinctively that he could retrieve, after a moment's thought, any volume in the room.

On the desk, which he bought because it looked like something a writer ought to have but which he can never bring himself to use, is the stack of psychoanalytic studies of creativity that includes such somber titles as Freud's *Beyond the Pleasure Principle* and Norman Holland's *The Dynamics of Literary Response*. On the floor beside the desk is a pile of paperbound volumes, mostly cheap mysteries that he checks out of the city library in bunches very much at random. The mystery novel is a new interest, and the pile has grown considerably in recent weeks.

Surveying the covers of the books scattered about—*The Films of Alfred Hitchcock*, *The Baseball Encyclopedia*, a Walker Percy novel, a study of Elizabethan stage conventions, a thin paperback featuring a naked female corpse—one might very well conclude that Cory is an unsystematic reader with wide-ranging interests and questionable taste. It is true; he is an amateur reader. Although he recognizes a distinction between William Faulkner and Dashiel Hammett, he savors both, and in fact once argued in an unpublished essay that Faulkner was essentially a mystery writer, admittedly of a very high order.

It's the absence of discrimination in his taste, Jack Abbott once told him, that has kept him from becoming a serious critic. Cory had wondered aloud if anybody at the university ever mentioned reading his articles. "One or two," Abbot had said. "They think you're a little crazy. One minute you're talking about *The Sun also Rises*, the next minute you're in the middle of a baseball novel." Cory had responded only with the observation that *Bang the Drum Slowly* was somewhat under-rated as a novel, but he knew Abbott was right. He will never be a scholar, although it doesn't bother him very much. They do it because it's their job. He does it because he loves it. He *was* an amateur, he had reminded Abbott at the time, from the Latin *amator*, lover.

Sitting in his litter of books on Monday evening with a glass of George Dickel on ice, Cory studies the box scores in the afternoon paper. The Cardinals had lost 7-4 to the Braves. He glances back at the league standings. Three games out. It's early in the season but the signs are clear—St. Louis possesses a potent offense, but they're in desperate need of relief pitching, most especially a closer. They're losing in the late innings. The Braves had scored five runs in the last two innings off three relievers.

He methodically reconstructs the game. Any knowledgeable fan can do it with relative accuracy, and even if you're wrong in some details you'll never know. "Baseball," Cory has written somewhere, "is the only game that offers anything approaching the intellectual satisfaction of the box score. It is the only game that can be enjoyed in the absence of the event itself."

His friends, when he had friends, were always mystified by his attachment to the game and, more particularly, by his devotion to the St. Louis Cardinals. It clearly has nothing to do with regional pride; St. Louis is a city foreign to him. It might as well be Lincoln, Nebraska, and what baseball fans there are in East Tennessee follow the Braves. But there it is every night when he turns to the sports section. A one-sided loss irritates him, but it is the easiest to take. The loss of a game they should have taken depresses him. A win gives him an inexplicable sense of well-being.

His link with the Cardinals had in fact been forged in childhood during the long summers at his grandparents' place in West Tennessee. It was after his mother died, and he was shipped out every June to the farm near Dyersburg, across the river from Missouri. At night and on Sunday afternoons he and his grandfather would listen to the Cardinal broadcast. He told him stories about the great players of the past, Musial, Enos "Country" Slaughter, and the shortstop Marty Marion. He remembers, after so many years, the old man standing in the middle of the living room to show him Musial's awkward-graceful batting crouch, like a coiled snake ready to strike.

He sits with the newspaper in his lap staring at the far wall, then reaches down beside the chair for a spiral notebook with a pen wedged in the metal ring. He looks down at the blank page for a time and then begins to write.

(Notes for Chapter VII)

1. Begin with Heywood Hale Broun's statement that baseball is "a shared delusion." Offer an explanation for this. Emphasize the pastoral elements of the game—the green field in the middle of the city, young boys brought up from the farm teams playing in old-fashioned knickers and stockings.

2. Bring in baseball's veneration for the past, statistics as a link between past and present, the sense of nostalgia for a time of lost innocence.

3. Speculate on the mythic elements. The object of the game is to return home. The home run is the ecstatic moment in baseball. Bring in the Bobby Thompson home run, perhaps the single most fabled event in the game.

He stops and takes a sip of the Dickel, then returns to the notebook, recognizing that he has steered himself into a slight difficulty.

4. Try to take into account the defensive elements of the game, which don't seem to fit the homecoming myth. Draw distinctions between defensive skill and offensive myth. We revere the great hitter who is an indifferent fielder, but the great fielder who can't hit is only the utility man.

He glances at the newspaper beneath the notebook in his lap. The double column of box scores holds his eye.

5. Somewhere work in the fact that baseball is the only game that can be fully reported in six square inches of newsprint. Perhaps the detective work of reconstructing the game from box scores could be a transition to Chapter VIII on the mystery novel.

6. Note for Chapter VIII—follow up on Robert O'Brian's argument about the mystery novel. Why is the ending of a mystery novel always a disappointment? O'Brian's answer: Because the explanation brings us back to the real world, the commonplace. A mystery is only a prolonged evasion of the real, an opportunity for infinite possibility.

While he is reading over what he has written the phone rings, and he closes the notebook and inserts the pen in the spiral binding. As he gets up the newspaper slides from his knees and floats to the floor, and he momentarily catches something vaguely familiar and disturbing, a photograph, as it spreads over the carpet.

"Yes?"

"Bob, this is Michael O'Connor. How are you?" O'Connor is the only person he knows who calls him Bob. He evidently assumes that anybody named Robert is automatically called Bob, and Cory has never bothered to correct him.

"Fine, Chancellor." Standing at the desk, he tries to focus on the paper, the photograph that caught his eye.

"I understand you're still plugging away in the library. I hope your research is going well."

"I appreciate the parking permit."

"No problem. Let me know if you need anything else."

"I will." It's in the section called *Living Today*. A photograph. Two women in swimsuits.

"You may have heard about the unfortunate incident over here."

"I heard some talk in the library. Said a dean had been killed?"

"A dean? Is that what they're saying? Hell, I wish it had been a dean. We've got deans who could disappear for months without anybody taking notice. No, it wasn't a dean. Did you know Hollis Sanders, the head of our English Department?"

"I don't believe I've met him."

"He was found dead in his office this morning."

"I'm sorry to hear it."

"We're all very much concerned, of course. Sanders was a scholar of some renown. International reputation. I'm sure you're familiar with his work." Cory is not. He moves away from the desk and stands over the newspaper, looking down at the photograph.

"Are you still there?"

"Sorry. I was distracted for a moment. No, I'm not familiar with Dr. Sanders' scholarship."

"Renaissance scholar. Has an edition of the plays of one of the

Jacobean dramatists, I believe. Can't remember which. Of course he was best known here for his work as an administrator—a real professional." Cory returns to the desk, sits down, and swings his feet up.

"Of course the entire university community is stunned. It goes without saying, but there is also the matter of the, ah, distasteful aspect of the thing. And other complications." O'Conner pauses but Cory does not respond.

"In fact, we've got a little problem over here, and I was wondering if you could help us out."

"I'd certainly be glad to do what I can."

"You may know that we have our own very fine campus police organization."

"I know there's a campus police force."

"And for some time now we've had an implicit if unofficial agreement with the city that we would investigate our own internal affairs. The city police, as a rule do not come on campus except for traffic control during sporting events. Our policemen and detectives have the same legal authority granted to any law enforcement officer."

"I didn't know that." *But then who gives a damn? Where's he going with this?*

"All of our policemen go to the state police academy in Murfreesboro for their training."

"I'm sure they're well trained."

"Well now it seems we have a small dispute. The campus police are accustomed to handling accident reports, robberies, drugs, such as that, but we've never had a"—he pauses for a beat—"well, a murder on campus. Our campus detectives—very competent men—began the investigation immediately on being called this morning, but now the city authorities believe that we should give it to them."

And of course they're right, Cory thinks. But he says nothing.

"I think we've got a compromise worked out that's acceptable to both sides. Both groups will work on the investigation. Our people will handle the campus work, the city police everything else. What we need is a neutral party to work out of my office to coordinate the whole thing."

"Coordinate? In what sense?"

"We'll be getting reports, depositions and so on from both sides. We need somebody to put all this together, keep everybody informed, keep me informed, prepare statements for the press. You know, that sort of thing."

"Why not just let the campus police report to the city police?"

"Well, that's the whole point, isn't it? We—that is, the university—do not wish to surrender complete control of this case to the city. We'd like to keep it as a kind of joint effort. The coordinator would be acting as my representative, but we wanted a neutral party. He would not of course participate in the actual investigation."

"I see."

"I realize it's unusual, but this is an unusual situation."

"And you're suggesting me for the job."

"We had a difficult time with that. We felt it could not be someone from the administration, but someone who has, let us say, an outside connection with the university."

"And you're proposing that I do it."

"Your name was arrived at after a great deal of deliberation." He waits for a response.

"Chancellor, does it not occur to you that this is a very inefficient way to investigate a crime, two separate agencies working independently with an amateur like me in the middle?"

It is only as he articulates it that he begins to see the element in the plan that identifies it with the Michael J. O'Connor he knows. "Is there some reason you don't *want* a thorough investigation?"

There is silence on the other end. Cory is conscious of a sigh. Then O'Connor comes back with a voice that is familiar to him. It's the conspiratorial voice Cory has heard in the board room whenever O'Connor attempts to gain the allegiance of the businessmen on the Development Council by feeding them the harmless little secrets of the inner world of the university. It's a voice that says *I am telling you this because you too are a man of the world. You know how these things are. I will tell you the real story of the little incident in the athletic dorm, but in return you must accept the responsibility of being on the inside. You are one of us.*

"Bob, you're a bright young man, and that's one of the reasons I agreed with the decision to ask you to handle this. But more important you're a person of integrity, and I believe I can confide in you. We've got a real crisis here. There are people who are out to nail us in any way they can. If Sanders' death turns into a full-blown scandal, we could be dealt a blow it would take us years to recover from."

"Do you have any reason to believe there *is* a scandal there?"

"I'll put it to you this way—I operate on the principle that the worst possible result will occur. In this case the worst possible result would be that there's something rotten in that department that an investigation will uncover."

Cory is aware that O'Connor has not answered his question. *He knows something he's not telling me.* "Chancellor, I appreciate the offer, but I'm not the man for a job like this. You must have a hundred people over there who would be much more qualified than I am."

"As I thought I made clear, we did not want to appoint an insider."

"Still—"

"Bob, I don't think you quite understand me. If I wanted to cover this thing up, I wouldn't have called you. Let me tell you exactly what I want, and you can be the judge. I want a little time—say three weeks—and I want some control over what gets released to the public. That's all I want, and that's what I'm hoping to get with this arrangement. After that let the chips fall where they may."

"Why three weeks?"

"In three weeks—assuming no complications—our budget will be set and the legislature will be adjourned. A year from now this whole thing will be forgotten."

"How are you going to get the police department to buy this cockeyed scheme?"

"They've already accepted it."

"Deathridge accepted it?"

"Well, I may have exaggerated just a bit the university's role in the investigation. What Deathridge agreed to was that the campus police would "participate" in the investigation. That was his term, deliberately vague I think. But more important, he agreed that we could compose the press releases. I think you can see what I was after."

"Still, I'm a little surprised."

"Deathridge is a friend of the university and an avid football fan. I believe he's a friend of yours also."

"I wouldn't put it that way. We were in school together. But I'm going to have to say no—"

"One more thing and then I'm through. You'll have nothing to do with the investigation except for the timing—and perhaps the phrasing—of public statements. Your job will simply be to put together a daily comprehensive report that's turned into my office. And an occasional short press release which is turned in to me."

"I'm sorry—"

"We'll give you an office over here, everything you need."

"Chancellor—"

"This is a very routine thing, no different really from one of your Development Council committees, and I don't know why you're blowing it out of proportion. There's no need for you even to see the people involved."

"Chancellor, I appreciate your calling me, but I have to decline. Of course I'll keep this conversation confidential."

"You're sure you wouldn't like to sleep on it tonight?"

"I'm sure."

"Dammit, you were the ideal man for the job. You could have had some credibility."

"I'm sorry to let you down."

"Is there some particular objection you have? We might be

able to accommodate your concern."

"Nothing in particular," Cory says. "I just don't see myself as the front man for a criminal investigation."

"Maybe you're right. Maybe I should just drop the whole thing and take it like a man." O'Connor seems more hurt than angry. "Maybe I should go back to teaching history and let the university go down the drain. Maybe Sanders committed suicide by hitting himself over the head with a fucking statue and the whole thing will blow over. I'll be talking to you."

The line goes dead before Cory can respond. He replaces the phone and turns back to the scattered newspaper, looking down at the photograph of two women in bathing suits standing in front of a large beach umbrella. The blonde on the left has her hands on her hips and is smiling self-consciously into the camera. The other woman seems unaware of the camera as she is caught brushing back her dark hair from her face. He bends down to read the caption. *Two styles you may be seeing around the pool this summer, shown here by Cynthia Price (left) and Sally Cory.*

The silence in the room seems oppressive as he retrieves the scattered newspaper. He returns to his chair, folds the page into a small square around the photograph and sits looking at it. The grainy texture of the newsprint gives the figure in the white swimsuit an almost pornographic quality. The dark shadows emphasize the separation of the breasts, the curve of the crotch, but the attitude of the head, the eyes, distance her from the viewer, render her inaccessible.

He flips the folded page across the floor, leans back in the chair, and lets his gaze sweep the room—the plate on the coffee table with the remains of a sandwich and an empty beer bottle, the sofa covered with magazines and newspapers, the dark television screen, the ragged stacks of books, the grainy photograph on the floor of two beautiful nearly-naked women, the notebook beside the chair with a pen wedged in the spiral ring. He bends down and picks it up, reads over what he has written, then tears the pages from the book and crumples them into a ball. He gets up, walks across the room, and stands looking down at the woman in the white bathing suit, thinking of something she once said to him: *Why is your instinct always to say no to whatever comes your way? Is that little world you live in so wonderful after all?*

"Boring actually," he says aloud, still staring at the photograph. "You always had me pegged."

He moves to the desk, locates the number and dials. The phone rings several times. *Gone out, he thinks, or gone to bed.*

"This is Michael O'Connor."

"Chancellor, am I allowed to change my mind on the favor you asked? I may have been a bit hasty in saying no." He tosses the paper ball idly as he speaks.

"So you're on board? That's great news."

"One condition. I need a letter signed by you authorizing my appointment. Whatever you want to call it."

"No problem."

"When do you want me to start?"

"Be here at ten tomorrow morning and we'll fill you in."

"Will I be working directly with you?"

"We haven't quite figured that out—all of this is unprecedented of course. May I ask what made you change your mind?"

"I'm not sure." He drops the ball into the wastebasket beside the desk. *But maybe it has something to do with trying to break out of a decade-long depression.*

"Whatever the reason, you're doing us a real service, and let me say there are very few people connected with the university I would trust in such a situation."

"Thank you." *Whatever the reason, it's almost certainly a mistake.*

"By the way, Bob, you may want to look at today's paper. There's a photograph of your ex-wife in the fashion section."

"Yes, I saw it."

"She's a beautiful woman."

Breathtaking, he thinks. He feels a curious sense of elation, as if the Cardinals have pulled one out in the bottom of the ninth.

TUESDAY

CHAPTER FOUR
THE PHYSICAL EVIDENCE

Tuesday morning at Stockton Tower is not what he expected. He expected to be greeted by the handsome-older-woman secretary, escorted into the Chancellor's spacious office, and after an exchange of pleasantries, receive a folder (marked *Confidential*, perhaps) which succinctly outlined his duties for the coming days.

What he gets is a youngish academic named James Houghton, who points him down the hall away from O'Connor's office. "The Chancellor asked me to stand in for him. He's going to be tied up for a while."

"Fine." Houghton, with an unguarded boyish look, strikes him immediately as a less devious executive type. He projects an efficient image, jacket-less, with a loosened tie and rolled up shirt sleeves. His image is marred only by a folded sheet of paper extending from his shirt pocket.

"It's not much of an office, I'm afraid." Houghton unlocks a door at the end of the hall and hands over the key. "It was being used for storage and the Chancellor had it cleared out yesterday when the Sanders thing came up." Among the several terms for their current crisis, *the Sanders thing* will come to dominate among those involved, perhaps because it is sufficiently vague and inclusive enough to include both the murder and its aftermath.

"You won't be distracted by the view." Houghton flips on the lights. "Sorry we couldn't do better for you."

Cory now sees that the room is without windows. It is the size of a small bedroom, and its furnishings consist of a wooden desk and a swivel chair. On the desk are two stacks of manila folders, a pile of pens, several yellow legal pads, and a laptop. Cory walks behind the desk, starts to take off his jacket, then seeing there's no place to hang it, leaves it on. He sits down tentatively and swings the chair from side to side.

Houghton clears his throat. "I'll make a list of things you need. The Chancellor didn't know about your work habits."

"This'll do fine—I don't think I'll need the computer. I've never owned one actually, as incredible as that must seem to somebody who probably spends half his day in front of one."

Houghton nods. "Most academics think they couldn't get along without one."

"Maybe you have somebody who can type up the reports."

"Of course." He reflects a moment on the request. "Probably I'll do it myself since the Chancellor wants to maintain a degree of confidentiality. What else?"

"I'm not sure what it is exactly that I'm doing so it's hard to know what to ask for."

"You know about as much as I do, to tell you the truth." Houghton indicates a thin stack of folders on the desk. "This is what we have so far from Safety and Security—the campus people. Gives the details from the crime scene. The other stack is from the city police, mainly just the medical examiner's report faxed over this morning and an interview with Sanders' lawyer. As I understand it, you're to combine the two into one detailed account, and at appropriate times prepare a statement that can be released to the press. Is that what the Chancellor indicated to you?"

"More or less. Could I ask you a question? Is there something here I'm missing?"

"I don't think you're missing anything. Or if you are I am too. But I think it's exactly what it looks like. Maybe what you're missing is the Chancellor's obsession with our public image."

"He seems to be going to extraordinary lengths here to perform a very simple operation. Almost as if—"

"Well, that's the way the university works, isn't it? When a problem comes up you appoint a committee, and by the time the committee's ready to report everybody's moved on to something else. In this case I guess you're the committee."

"I see."

"Actually, the arrangement is much more ingenious than I realized at first. The Chancellor's not interfering with the investigation in any way. In fact, as he said this morning, it's progressing rapidly on two fronts. But of course the part you're involved in is not really an investigation, it's public relations. Both the city and the campus police have been instructed to refer any inquiries to the coordinator or to our office. What he's gained though this little setup is control over what gets released to the public. But you've probably figured that out."

"Something like that."

Houghton's gesture takes in the bare room. "A little confining, but you shouldn't have to be in here more than a couple of hours a day. After you've finished there's no reason you can't go on about your business. The Chancellor said you were doing some work in the library. I'll come down when you're through and collect whatever you need typed up. Just leave it here on the desk. I've got a key."

"What if somebody asks me about the investigation? What am I free to tell them?"

"You're free to give them anything in the press releases—after they've been cleared by O'Connor. He said you agreed to that last night."

"I don't remember that coming up, but I'm not complaining. I could say that I've been had except that I pretty much saw the way the wind was blowing last night."

Houghton's look asks *then why did you agree to it?*

He has no answer. *I could say that last night I sat alone in my big house on Cherokee Boulevard and contemplated the pulpy photograph of a woman's body I once knew quite intimately. I could say that I am bored with myself, my work, my good chair, my good books, my life in perfect order.* "Did he send the letter I asked for?" Cory guesses he's looking at it.

Houghton produces the folded sheet from his shirt pocket. Above O'Connor's dated signature there is one sentence: *Effective this date Robert Cory will coordinate the university's internal investigation into the circumstances surrounding the death of Dr. J. Hollis Sanders.*

"That okay?"

"Well, it does put a little different slant on it—I mean, the implication here is that I'm conducting an internal investigation quite apart from the official one."

"That's actually pretty close to what you're doing. I think when the Chancellor had to put it down in black and white he realized that you could have no legal standing in the investigation. You're the university's representative in the investigation."

"The Chancellor's stand-in."

"You could put it that way. Anything else I can help you with?"

"Did you know him? Sanders?"

Houghton seems surprised by the question. "Not really. Just meetings, university business—routine stuff. We didn't run in the same circles."

"What sort of a man was he?"

"I'm not sure exactly what you're asking."

"I guess I'm asking what sort of man gets murdered in his office. Was he murdered because of who he was, or was he just in the wrong place at the wrong time? If I knew more about him, would I have certain suspicions? That's what I'm asking."

Cory hears a faint ring, and Houghton pulls a cell phone from a pants pocket and studies the screen. "Sorry, I need to take this." He puts it to his ear. "Yes, just showing him to his office, such as it is." A pause. "Nothing at the moment. Talk to you in a few minutes." He clicks off. "The Chancellor checking on us."

"So back to my question."

"Yes. What sort of man gets murdered in his office? I'm not sure I can answer that question, but I can tell you this. If somebody asked me to guess which of our department heads just made the evening news, I would probably say Hollis Sanders."

"The reason being?"

"He was a very flamboyant man whose social life was not confined to his university colleagues. He was moderately wealthy—family money I think—good-looking, athletic, divorced. According to the stories I've heard, he was attracted to beautiful women and everything else that goes with the good life. I've seen him at several university functions with some real stunners. Never the same one, as I recall. Also according to the stories, he drank to excess, which concerned the Chancellor somewhat, not to mention rumors of drugs. But then there was more gossip about Hollis Sanders than the rest of the university administration combined. I'm sure you'll hear some of it."

"That explains a lot."

"You mean this little arrangement the Chancellor has devised."

"He's hoping to squelch any hint of scandal."

"That would be a reasonable conclusion, but I'm not going to speculate."

"It's not so much the crime itself, but what it might uncover. That's what he wants control over."

"I don't think I want to get any further into the Chancellor's motives." Houghton consults his watch. "Anything else?"

"Not at the moment."

"Then I'll leave you to your work."

Whatever that is. It is my lot to play the amateur in a world of professionals. Houghton closes the door behind him.

Alone in the windowless room with a legal pad and a stack of documents he is, he realizes, back in his element. He leans back in the swivel chair, puts his feet on the desk, and opens the first folder.

In a little less than an hour he has finished his summary. He rereads it once then tears the pages from the legal pad, numbers them, and slides them to the corner of the desk. When he gets up from his chair, he has reached several conclusion. First, the investigation so far has produced not the slightest glimmer of a clue as to who might have killed J. Hollis Sanders. Second, illiteracy is rampant among law enforcement officers. Third, he has been somewhat hasty in his initial reaction that only a romantic illusion could concoct fascinating mysteries from the death of a college administrator. In fact, he is intrigued by the whole situation. He has to remind himself, however, that he is still in the opening pages of the mystery novel, as it were, when everything is unknown and the imagination is fired by possibilities. It can only be later, if the truth emerges, that the validity of his theory will be tested.

As he stands by the desk another idea takes hold of him. He hesitates a moment, then sits down and begins a longer second set of notes, this one for himself. It takes him another half hour, and when he's finished, he reads through them again to see if he's missed something.

> *1. Sanders was killed, in all likelihood, sometime after 6 p. m. on the Friday night before the beginning of spring break. The condition of the body makes it impossible to pinpoint it more exactly. The secretary, Margaret Bains, left about 5:30 with Sanders still alive—but could the murder have occurred a good deal later? Was it his habit to work late? Were there other English faculty in the building after 5:30?*
>
> *2. The campus police report suggests the possibility of an interrupted burglary, but in fact there were no signs of a break-in. Nothing from the office was taken (with one possible exception), and there were two relatively new computers in the outer office. Sanders' wallet, containing more than a hundred dollars in cash and several credit cards, was found on his body.*
>
> *3. Because of the upcoming break, the building and elevators were locked at 6:00. The outer door of the English Office was also locked by the secretary when she left at 5:30. The entrances to the building and the elevators can be unlocked by punching in*

a code (which is apparently given out freely), but not the English Office. Only Sanders, the associate head, the secretaries, and the custodians officially have keys, although Margaret Bains believes that there are a number of duplicate keys floating about, since Sanders sometimes had them made for people whom he met in the office after hours. Does that mean that Sanders knew the killer(s)? Who is the associate head?

4. The murder weapon was quite possibly a tennis trophy, not in fact a "fucking statue," as the Chancellor suggested in his call on Monday evening. Ms. Bains reported that to her knowledge the only object missing from the office was a heavy cut glass bowl perhaps ten to twelve inches high and at least a foot in diameter mounted on a thick wooden base. Etched in the glass was the figure of a male tennis player along with the inscription "Knoxville Open Championship 1995." According to Ms. Bains, Sanders kept this bowl (filled with candy, which he offered to visitors) on his desk—presumably as a gesture which simultaneously made light of his tennis prowess and showed it off. Tiny shards of glass consistent with the trophy were found in the carpet, along with numerous chocolate nougats. The assumption is that the bowl was broken when Sanders was struck with it, and the killer took with him the broken pieces and the wooden base. (Presumably because of possible fingerprints.) Inspector Owen Battles of the campus police initially wondered if the bowl was substantial enough to kill a man; Mrs. Bains assured him that it was.

5. According to the autopsy, Sanders received two blows to the head which produced wounds of

different configurations. The medical examiner suggests he was struck with a blunt object, then fell, striking the corner edge of the low glass-top table beside which the body was found. He theorizes that it was the second head wound, from the table, that proved fatal. (Seems like an absurd way to go, but the actor William Holden went the same way.) There was a great deal of blood, and presumably the assailant would have had blood on his clothing. The blood type was AB.

6. Although he was not seen by anyone for ten days, there was no suspicion about his absence. Sanders was divorced, no children. He lived alone in a high-end gated community in West Knoxville.

7. The vacuuming of the carpet to retrieve the glass particles produced one unexpected result. Traces of a white powder, possibly cocaine, were found in the carpet near the table. On the table also were an almost-full bottle of single malt scotch and two glasses. Two chairs were pulled up to the table. Whatever else this indicates, it explains a lot about the Chancellor's actions of late.

8. The campus police report laments the paucity of physical evidence—no sign of a break-in, no witnesses, no apparent trace left behind by the assailant. A paper coffee cup from McDonald's found on Sanders' desk was later determined to have been left by Inspector Hutchins of the campus police.

9. Fourteen latent fingerprints and one palm print were lifted, but no results on this. The campus report was especially interested in possible prints on the two glasses. Elimination prints are to be collected by the campus police.

10. Who profits financially from Sanders'

death? Apparently no one here. His attorney contacted the city police yesterday. Sanders' entire estate, which is considerable, goes to a half-sister in California with whom he is on good terms. Nothing suspicious there.

11. Inspector Battles of the campus police seems to be operating on the premise that the accumulation of physical evidence leads to the solution of the crime. Is it possible to reconstruct the crime from the physical evidence in the same way that a baseball game may be reconstructed from the box scores? Possibly, but then maybe it's better to find out who did it first, then look for evidence.

He tears the pages of notes from the pad, folds them, and slips them into the inside pocket of his jacket. He looks at his watch. He swivels his chair slowly from side to side. The library, he decides, is out for the immediate future. His other decision was made about twenty minutes earlier without his really knowing it. He is going to stroll over to the Humanities Building and renew an old friendship—assuming that Jack Abbott is still a member of the English faculty. Surely he could tell some interesting stories about his dead department head.

CHAPTER FIVE
SAFETY AND SECURITY

Inspector Owen Battles, Campus Safety and Security, is not having a good morning. First he has learned that the autopsy report will be delayed, since it is being routed through somebody named Robert Cory. Now he is discovering in stages that the Chancellor might veto plans to fingerprint and interview the faculty of the English Department.

The word came down first in an email from Ira Coleman, Director of Safety and Security: *Is the fingerprinting really necessary? The Chancellor thinks the faculty might take offense.* When in the course of the ensuing conversation Coleman learned that he planned to take statements from the faculty as well, he said they would also have to clear that with O'Connor. Battles decides he has to talk to the Chancellor, locates the number and punches it in. The conversation ends in something of a draw.

"Sir, I believe I can make them understand that we *expect* to find their prints there. What we want to do is to identify the faculty prints so we can follow up on any others we find. Those are called elimination prints."

"I understand that, Owen. I'm just thinking about the indignity the faculty might feel at being fingerprinted. These are respectable people, scholars, national reputations. How will it look to them? I'm afraid we can't allow it."

Battles does not reply immediately. *We can't allow it.* This is not the first time the Chancellor has involved himself with a campus investigation, but earlier instances have been relatively minor, mostly involving student athletes. Can a Chancellor trump a murder investigation? Probably, Battles concludes, since his boss Ira Coleman reports directly to the Chancellor. He decides not to pursue it. "I'm sure, sir, that I could explain it to them," he says finally.

"No, I'm afraid it won't do. Don't you have anything else you can be working on?"

"We were going to start questioning the faculty this morning, but Ira said we'd have to check with you."

A pause. "What form would these interviews take?"

"Routine questions about Sanders, his recent activities, friends and so on."

"Is it absolutely necessary?"

"How would it look if we *don't* talk to them?"

O'Connor clears his throat. "The thing you must never forget is that these are very sensitive, perceptive people. They're accustomed to reading more into things than is actually there—they call it literary criticism. Your questioning must be without guile, perfectly straightforward and routine. You're asking them about Sanders, and that's all. You must never imply that anyone associated with the university could be implicated. You must never ask them leading questions or quarrel with their answers. Are you following me on this, Owen?"

"Yes, sir."

"And I want you to visit these people in their offices. Make them feel comfortable. You just happened to be in the building. Don't make a big fuss about it. Don't arrange an appointment. You can find out from the secretary when their office hours are, or they may be posted somewhere—I don't know. But you understand the kind of tone I want."

"Yes, sir."

"One more thing. I want you to do all the questioning yourself. Leave Hutchins out of it. Find him something to do that he can handle on his own. Keep him busy, but keep him away from anything important."

"I'll find something for him."

There are only the two of them—Battles and Hutchins, in addition to the dozen uniformed patrolmen. Battles had been a city policeman for fifteen years, attaining the rank of sergeant, when he was offered the post of Inspector with the campus police as a part of the university's attempt to upgrade Safety and Security. At the time the campus force was composed entirely of uniformed patrolmen. The title of Inspector was somewhat arbitrary—the Chancellor at that time, O'Connor's predecessor, thought it had a nice ring to it, perhaps because it sounded British.

Roy Hutchins was added a few years later, but he hadn't worked out very well. He came with high recommendations from somebody on the Knoxville force—Battles' guess was that they had wanted to unload him—and he had two years of college at some place in New Jersey, but he had trouble catching on to things and he dressed badly.

"Do you think, Owen, that you could delay the start of your interviews a day? We're having a sort of remembrance service for the faculty this afternoon. It'll take you several days, won't it, the interviews?"

"Yes, sir. I'll start Wednesday morning. Could I ask you one thing?" Battles' courage has been bolstered by the ease with which he has been permitted access to the English faculty. "I know you had good reason for appointing this man Robert Cory, but it's slowing things down. I need the autopsy report right now, but with the system we've got set up I won't get it until sometime tomorrow. Couldn't we have the Knoxville people send one copy of their stuff to me and one to your man? It would really help."

"Owen"—the Chancellor's voice sounds tired but with infinite patience—"we've gone over it. This is the very best I could get out of them. I know it's an awkward arrangement, but I think we're extremely lucky to have reached this point. Do you realize that five years ago we wouldn't have had this opportunity? We've come a long way."

"Yes, sir, but there are complications. Like the fingerprints. The physical evidence is just not—"

"Fuck the physical evidence. We're not fingerprinting the English Department."

"Yes, sir, I'll keep in touch."

"I know that you will, Owen. We'll just have to do the best we can with what we've got. I'm depending on you."

"I understand. We'll do what we can."

Hanging up the phone, Battles reaches for his notebook and makes two brief entries: *Start with the English faculty on Wed. morning. Find something for Hutchins to do.* He leafs through his earlier notes, looking for something to occupy his time for the rest of the morning. There is a rendering of the murder scene, the crudely sketched outline of the body by the coffee table resembling a child's drawing. There are notes of his conversation with the security man of the dorm complex across the street from the Humanities Building, descriptions of cars parked in the area the night of the murder. When he comes to the list of phone numbers he stops.

Nosing around Sanders' office on Monday afternoon after the body and the worst of the smell had been removed, Battles noticed that the victim had been in the habit of jotting down phone numbers with initials on the cover of his telephone directory. Battles had copied them out:

> FC 974-2989
> AC 974-4481
> HR 588-9061
> SC 588-2173
> PG 983-2011
> JA 588-6073

Now in the absence of anything else to pursue he decides to dial them, and starts down the list. FC turns out to be the Faculty Club, AC the Liberal Arts Advising Center. HR is Harry's, a restaurant in West Knoxville. SC proves more promising when a woman's voice responds. Battles identifies himself, informs her that her telephone number has been recovered from a crime scene, and asks for her name.

"Cynthia Price. What is this about?"

It doesn't match, but okay. "I'm not at liberty to discuss the details of the case at this point. And your address?"

He copies the name and address in the notebook, hesitates, then decides not to pursue it further at the moment, since he doesn't quite know what route to take. He tells her that he will be back in touch, and after he has hung up reflects that Cynthia Price seemed remarkably calm about her phone number being found at the scene of a crime. He is dialing the next number, PG, when Roy Hutchins walks in. He is wearing a shirt that looks vaguely Hawaiian.

"Sanders' car's in the parking garage of the Humanities Building. Been there for the whole week. What are we suppose to do with it?"

"Just leave it there for the time being. There *is* something you could do, though. Go over to Plants and Grounds and find out who was assigned to clean the English offices—what their schedule was the last couple of weeks and so on. Find out if anybody was up there the Friday before the break."

"Anything else?"

"Ira's not going to let us fingerprint the English Department. The Chancellor doesn't think it would look good."

Hutchins, not a dedicated criminologist, shrugs.

"Did you look through the car?"

"Pretty clean. Usual stuff in the glove compartment and this lipstick." Hutchins sets the tube on the desk. "Nice car. Think the family wants to sell it?"

Battles is looking at the lipstick on his desk. Physical evidence. Be nice if it turns out to belong to Cynthia Price of 7519 Bardon Drive. When he looks up, Hutchins is gone. He goes back to his telephone numbers.

PG is the Parker Gallery on Homberg Drive. He enters that in the notebook just because he doesn't know what to make of it. They sell paintings and jewelry and do framing, he recalls. JA, the last number, leads him to another woman's voice, this one deep and throaty. A very sensuous voice.

"Is this 588-6073?"

"It is."

"This is Safety and Security at Western Appalachian University. I need to inform you that your telephone number was recovered from a crime scene. Could I have your name please?"

"May I have *your* name?"

"This is Inspector Owen Battles."

"Well, Inspector Battles—if that is your real name—I'm going to hang up now and make a phone call. I don't believe that real policemen operate in this manner." She's gone.

Battles replaces the phone slowly, feeling like a criminal. In his notebook he draws a large question mark beside the initials JA. He will discover the owner of that wonderfully sensuous voice a bit later by more conventional means, but for the moment Janice Abbott has proven too cagey for him.

CHAPTER SIX
THE INTERIM HEAD

He locates the office on the third floor of the Humanities Building. The hallway bears the faint scent of disinfectant and something else he can't quite place. The office door is ajar and Jack Abbott, on the telephone, spots him and motions him in. Abbott gives him a long-suffering look to indicate the nature of his conversation and points him to a chair, keeping his eyes on him as he waits for a chance to interrupt what is evidently an unbroken monologue on the other end. There is a look in his eyes Cory does not remember. He has the vague, uncertain gaze of a man walking away from a traffic accident.

The room is large and more elaborately furnished than he would have thought customary with faculty offices. The leather couch and conference table suggest that Abbott is now an administrator of some order. As he sits looking around the office, Abbott is attempting with little success to break into the conversation, "Look—" He stops and rolls his eyes at Cory. "Look, Charles—" He hold the phone away from his ear and sighs. "Look, Charles, I'm sure there's a good reason you were moved out of Area 9. Where *is* Area 30?" A pause. "Jesus, that's on the other side of the stadium. You're going to have a long walk."

Cory's gaze moves across the book case—*A Reader's Guide to T. S. Eliot, T. S. Eliot: A Memoir, Selected Prose of T. S. Eliot.* Abbott's field is modern poetry but, as Cory recalls, he has never published much—an article here and there, but the Eliot book he used to talk about apparently never appeared.

"Why don't you just move into the parking garage in the

building?" Another pause. "I didn't know there was a waiting list. You seem to be up a creek." He grins uneasily at Cory. "Can't we wait until tomorrow to straighten this out? We've got that service this afternoon if you'll recall." A grimace. "Oh, really? Don't you think you ought to show a little respect? Jesus, that's a very harsh thing to say. I know you weren't on very good terms, but Jesus." His gaze stays on Cory and he slowly shakes his head. "Look, I've got to get off now. I've got somebody in the office. Talk to you tomorrow."

"Charles Durrell," he says, replacing the phone. "A real pain in the ass. Here we are in the middle of a crisis and he's distraught because he got moved out of his parking space. Jesus. That's the kind of thing you deal with in this job—parking spaces. People think we're over here grappling with intellectual issues, poetry, art. No, it's parking spaces." He sits back in his chair, trying to recover. "Well, how the hell are you? It's been a long time." His voice sounds hollow.

"A long time. You seem to have come up in the world." Cory's gesture takes in the large office. "Is this where my tax dollars are going?"

"For the last two years I've served as the English Department's Associate Head." He bears down on the last two words cynically to indicate he is not impressed with the title, and Cory mentally checks off one of the questions he had earlier posed to himself. *Who is the associate head?* The answer, astonishingly enough, is Jack Abbott.

"Unfortunately, due to circumstances beyond my control I have just been appointed Interim Head. It sounds like one of those temporary toilets they rent out to construction sites, like that company you inherited. Remember that?"

Cory smiles but there's no humor in Abbott's voice. He looks very tired and a little jittery. Perhaps he's bearing the burden of the unusual situation that has just developed in his department. Whatever the cause, he does not appear to Cory to be up to handling it.

"So you'll be moving into the main office?"

"As soon as it ceases to be a crime scene, as Inspector Battles calls it, and they get the smell out. I guess you've heard about it." Abbott fiddles with some papers on his desk. "What are you doing over here? The last time we talked you told me to go to hell, as I recall."

"It was about Sally, you'll also recall. I was maybe a bit too defensive about the divorce. I hope you haven't held a grudge all this time." *He doesn't know. Shouldn't O'Connor have informed him? Should I tell him?* "Actually, the Chancellor has me doing some busywork connected with your department head's death. I'm sort of a one-man committee."

Abbott is suddenly attentive. "What's he up to now?"

"I'm supposed to be coordinating the university's internal investigation, whatever that means. What it amounts to is a lot of paper shuffling. I think he's trying to cover all the bases." It doesn't sound very convincing, but then he reflects that it's actually the truth.

"A careful man," Abbott says. He keeps his eyes on Cory. "You're an unlikely type for a job like that."

"That was my first reaction. I think he wants to keep it out of his office as much as possible. I don't completely understand it, to tell you the truth."

"How did he find you, of all people?"

"He knows me from the Development Council."

"You're friends."

"No, not at all. I'm somebody he sees every three months with a bunch of businessmen. I'm sure you know him better than I do."

Abbott starts to respond, thinks better of it, and then says quietly, "It's a hell of a note."

"It's not something that happens every day." Cory sees that Abbott is as uncomfortable as he is. "How's Janice?"

"Oh, fine." The tone is so unconvincing that Cory decides there must be something terribly wrong with Janice. "She'll be delighted to hear you're back."

"You make it sound as if I've been out of the country."

"Well, you know what I mean."

They fall silent, and he, Cory, sees himself as Jack Abbott must see him from across the desk, an outsider, playing a part in the Sanders affair he hasn't earned, clueless. "I just wanted to come over and let you know I was around. Maybe we can have lunch one day."

"Sure. I'm tied up today but maybe one day this week. So you're back in polite society?"

Cory nods. *What is it about this man that makes him seem so different? Is the Jack Abbott of my memory a trick of my imagination? Have I invented him?*

"Did you learn anything in your absence?" Abbott is looking out the window.

"I learned that I'm easily bored with myself." *And that I still have a mindless devotion to Sally, whom you may remember as my wife.*

"Could I entice you to come over to the house for dinner one night? I'm sure Janice would love to see you."

"Sure. Why not?" It would be disillusioning to discover that Janice too is nothing more than a creature of his fantasy.

"I'll give you a call." Abbott stands up from the desk to end the conversation, but Cory holds on for a moment.

"Could I ask you something?"

"Go ahead."

"I get the impression from O'Connor—just a faint impression— that he's afraid of something being uncovered in your department. Maybe I'm wrong but the feeling I get is that it's something as damaging—if it got out—as a murder. Do you know what I'm talking about?"

"No, I'm afraid I don't."

"I think it has to do with your late department head—at least the way he was described to me."

"What have you heard?"

"Nothing specific—just that there were a lot of rumors. You must have known him as well as anybody, being associate head."

"We were not particularly close," Abbott says.

"He was described to me as flamboyant."

Abbott nods. "Maybe we can talk about Hollis Sanders at some later point. I'm not inclined to at the moment."

"And you're not aware of anything in your department that the Chancellor would be concerned about?"

Abbott has turned from Cory and is looking out the window again. When he speaks, there is a shift in tone, an edge. Perhaps it's only the administrator's paternal voice, protecting his own. "Every department has its skeletons. I don't know that we have anything more than usual. People get drunk at parties and make passes at other people's wives. Is that what you're talking about? You used to live in the world. You should know about things like that."

"I don't think that's what I'm talking about. Maybe I'm wrong."

"We've also got more than our share of kooks. That fellow Durrell I was just talking to—if this were the sixties, he'd be out marching somewhere. As it is, he just yells a lot about the evils of our sedentary profession and makes everybody uncomfortable. He's always making the student paper. A couple of weeks ago at a faculty senate meeting he referred to the head of Women's Studies with what was deemed a sexist term."

"She in your department too?"

"Jennifer Reed."

"I got the impression from your end of the telephone conversation that Durrell and Sanders weren't the best of friends."

"Are you conducting an investigation?"

Cory laughs. "No, I'm just curious about your department. O'Connor pulled me into this, and I'm wondering what I've gotten myself into." *I don't think I'm conducting an investigation.*

"I'll just put it this way. Sanders and Durrell were on opposite sides of a continuing argument about the values of the profession, and Durrell didn't always play fair. Sanders has been trying to find a way to get rid of him—and Durrell knows that—but he couldn't because Charles is a very popular teacher, and he's got all the other credentials too—a book on Yeats that's very trendy."

"He's in your field?" Cory is reminded of Abbott's non-existent book on Eliot.

"Yes. Durrell is a legitimate crank, but he's the kind that finds a home in the university and even gains a following. He came here from Chapel Hill with great recommendations, but after he got tenure he suddenly shifted his sights. He wants to reform the university." Abbott offers the last observation as if it is evidence of Durrell's instability.

"And Sanders represented the Old Guard?"

"That's right."

"Well, you certainly wouldn't kill a man because of philosophical differences."

"*What are you talking about*? I certainly hope you're not implying that anybody in the department is in any way connected with this business. *Jesus*. Has O'Connor said something?"

"No. Certainly not. It just seemed to me that he was very nervous about your department, and you were the only person I knew to talk to."

"O'Connor may have gotten wind of a few stories about Sanders floating around campus. Nothing more than that. Look, Robert, I've got to get busy here. Why don't you come over one night this week? I'll get Janice to give you a call."

"Fine. She can reach me at home."

He gets up to leave, feeling foolish and wishing he hadn't come. Abbott walks him to the door, searching for a way to recover from his abruptness. He puts a hand on Cory's shoulder. "How's your work coming? Any new outrageous theories?"

Cory, grateful for the effort, smiles. "It's okay. I think I'm going to give it a rest. You know, driving home yesterday I was thinking about the summer evening you and Janice came over—when we lived in the Sequoyah Apartments—and I proposed the theory about women in cars."

"What do you mean *you*? That was *my* theory."

"No, you're wrong. I remember it very well. Sally, as I recall, took the whole thing personally and accused me of blatant sexism."

"That's not the way I remember it. In fact, it's made the rounds of cocktail parties all over West Knoxville. It's firmly identified with me."

"It's okay. If you want it you can have it. But it *was* mine."

"I think your imagination's playing tricks on you. Anyway, you've got hundreds of theories. You could let me have just one."

"It's yours."

They stand at the door grinning, almost recovering something, but then Abbott breaks the mood, perhaps with a certain malice. "Sally sleeping with anybody these days?"

"I'm not the one to ask. We don't talk." Cory turns to go.

"Did you see her picture in the paper last night? I bet every kid in Knoxville got a boner."

Who is this man? I don't know him.

Abbott sticks out his hand. "It's great to see you again."

"Good to see you, Jack."

But it isn't good, he knows, as he walks the halls of the Humanities Building looking at names on office doors.

CHAPTER SEVEN
THE LOYAL OPPOSITION

Killing time is the phrase that's stuck in his mind as he wanders the third-floor hall of the Humanities Building. He plays with the words as a title for the chapter on the mystery novel. *Killing Time: The Mystery Novel in American Fiction.* Too stuffy. *Killing Time: The Appeal of the Mystery Novel.* Better, but not quite right.

Killing time is what he's doing at the moment, he knows, distracting himself to avoid thinking about Jack Abbott. It has become a habit of mind over the last few years. Writing the book is killing time, distracting himself to avoid thinking about what? Sally? And this, whatever it is he's doing, killing time.

He walks slowly, pausing to read the name plates on the doors. T. Walter Press, Director of Composition. J. R. Fogle, Director of Undergraduate Studies. P. G. Litz, Director of Graduate Studies. Everybody on the third floor seems to have a title.

When he comes to the departmental office, he pauses. It is directly across from the elevator and, in the manner of modern office design, separated from the hallway only by a wall of glass panels. The occupants are on display, and Cory stands by the elevator and watches them. The secretary to the left he guesses is Margaret Bains, who discovered the body. She is plain and no doubt efficient. The young woman at the middle desk, a striking blonde, looks extremely inefficient. She was named in his morning report, but he can't call it up, Connie something. The desk on the right is unoccupied. The door behind Margaret Bains obviously leads to Sanders' office. It now bears a sign which announces in red letters: *No Admittance Beyond This Point By Order of Campus*

Police.

The two women are staring intently into their computer screens—business as usual—but their minds have to be fixed on the room behind the door. Cory has the impulse to go in, ask some meaningless question, engage them in conversation, but he resists it. Instead he imagines the scene that might have taken place almost two weeks earlier.

Say someone gets off the elevator here and approaches the office. The door is locked and the outer office where the secretaries now sit is probably dark, but there is a light on in Sanders' office that can be seen from the hall. He knocks on the door and Sanders comes out of his office, sees him in the lighted hall through the glass, and unlocks the door. They go through the dark outer office into Sanders' office, with his door left open. Or maybe he closes it. Maybe he turns on the lights in the outer office before he unlocks the door. Maybe Margaret Bains left them on when she departed at 5:30—that could be checked. Cory prefers his first reconstruction—dark outer office into Sanders' lighted office with his door left open.

There is nothing telling about this recreation except perhaps that Sanders would have seen his killer through the glass as he stood in the lighted hallway. And one other thing—a moment in which the murder is removed from police reports and placed in the world of time. It really happened. Somebody walked in there for reasons known only to himself at the moment. There was an argument, a fight, something. After it was over, he walked out, took this elevator down to the plaza and went home, or to the grocery, or somewhere in the world. And he's still out there watching television and reading the newspaper. Killing time.

Or *she* or *they*. Cory fishes the folded pages from inside his jacket and scribbles a note to himself. He has an idea on a sexual angle, and as if to announce it a bell rings above his head. But it's only the elevator, and an elderly gentleman exits and walks briskly down the hall. Cory holds the door open while he debates with himself. Why not? Perhaps somebody like Charles Durrell would be more forthcoming about the dirty little secrets of the department. He slips past the closing doors and ascends to the fourth floor.

Another cell block of offices, but these doors have no titles. The administrators in the department are obviously confined to the third floor. He arrives at the door inscribed with the name Charles Durrell and stops. Unlike the others, it is taped over with a jumble of newspaper clippings, cartoons, sheets giving directions to students. Cory bends down to look at one of the cartoons, a *New Yorker* type that pictures a professor standing in front of a large class. The caption says: "This is English 312, The Victorian Novel. I assume all of you can read." The cartoon moves away as the door swings open.

"Reading my door, are you?"

"Sorry." Cory straightens to look into the face of the speaker, who is maybe mid-forties, handsome, bearded. He vaguely resembles a young Castro, dressed in jeans, a blue work shirt, and a corduroy jacket.

"That's fine. I like to encourage reading at whatever level. Do I know you?"

"My name is Robert Cory and I was in the building—"

"Ah, I do know you. I read your Hemingway piece. I'm Charles Durrell." He sticks out his hand and they shake across the threshold.

Cory reflects for a moment. "I believe you're the first person I've ever run into who's read anything I wrote. I mean somebody who wasn't a friend."

"Good stuff. You have a weird mind. Of course you understand that much of it's wrong."

He says this with such matter-of-factness that Cory can only nod. Durrell continues. "But then you understand that what everybody writes is wrong, so the only thing you can hope for is to be wrong in an interesting way. All reading is necessarily misreading, as Nietzsche has informed us, but not all misreading is equal. Have you read Nietzsche?"

"'There are no facts, only interpretations.' He was one of my projects a couple of years ago." Cory has the sense of being back in the classroom, taking notes on Nietzsche's perspectivism. Durrell seems unaware that he's lecturing.

"You understand that this principle applies only to the sort of thing you and I do. There may be other writing that's not wrong, but I'm not interested in that. You're younger than I thought you'd be. Got a few minutes? Come in—I've been wanting to meet you."

That's strange, to think somebody's been wanting to meet him. "Thank you. I was just, well, killing time." He removes a pile of books from the one available chair and sits. Durrell leans against the desk.

"You want some coffee?" He points to a thermos on the desk.

Cory shakes his head. "Now that I think about it, there's a small problem with your theory. A critical approach that's based on the principle that all interpretation is wrong must itself fall into the same category. That is, according to your own principle, your theory is wrong."

"I see I'm dealing with a worthy opponent here." Durrell brightens. "You've uncovered a small complication, but there are ways around it. Nietzsche got around it by—" He's interrupted by the chime of a cell phone on his cluttered desk and after a short search locates it. "Yes? . . . no kidding . . . seems like a crazy thing to do . . . I wouldn't put it past him . . . I can't talk right now, call you back."

A look of irritation crosses his face as he turns back to Cory, but it fades quickly. "Now, what was I saying? To hell with it—doesn't matter. What brings you over here?"

"I was talking to Jack Abbott."

"Ah, yes. You used to be friends."

"A long time ago. How did you know?"

Durrell ignores the question. "Well, old Jack has come a long way in the last few years. My guess is he'll be the new department head."

"Does he have a lot of support?"

"Probably, but not from me. He's just an extension of Sanders.

Get rid of one—in a manner of speaking—and they zap in another one exactly like him. He's already trying to move me out of my parking place—all the way across campus. Can you believe that? I just confirmed that Abbott's the one behind it."

"Why would he want to do something like that?"

"He and Sanders have been on my case a good while now. Simple harassment." Durrell shrugs. "Well, as Freud once said, life is not easy."

"Do you mean they're trying to force you out?" Cory asks the question as innocently as possible. He has developed an interest in the inner workings of J. Hollis Sanders' department and appears to have stumbled onto a person who can tell him a great deal.

"Well, they can't fire me—I've got tenure. But they'd like me to leave of my own accord. I don't fit their image of the professional types they want in the department. I actually spend my time with students instead of traveling around the country going to meetings, talking to other professional types. In the jargon of the profession it's known as visibility, acquiring a national reputation. You know what Shaw said—a profession is a conspiracy against society. Anyway, I can't bring myself to play that role. Any fool can do that. I figure if anybody wants to know what I have to say they can find it in the library. But it's more than that. They don't care much for my style. I'm afraid I'm not very presentable. Hell, I'm talking as if Sanders were still alive. It's hard to get used to the idea that somebody finally did what a lot of us fantasized about."

"He was disliked in the department?"

"Well, he was not the meanest man I ever met, but he was right up there near the top."

"He had a lot of enemies."

"I wouldn't put it that way. He had too much power to have enemies, but a lot of people secretly hated his ass. I was one of a select few who openly hated his ass. Abbott can tell you about that." He pauses to look Cory in the eye. "Maybe he already has."

"Not exactly."

Cory notes the slightest shift in Durrell's manner. "You have some special interest in this?"

Looking back, Cory will fix on this moment as the beginning of an unlikely chain of events in the days to follow, and he will also conclude that his indiscretion was triggered by Durrell's candor, his complete ingenuousness. Whatever the reason, he impulsively reaches inside his jacket for O'Connor's letter and hands it to Durrell, who reads the one sentence and returns it. He shakes his head slowly.

"'Internal investigation?' I've got some old costumes out in the barn," Durrell says. "We can put on an investigation and save the school."

"I know. It's crazy."

"This university never ceases to amaze me. Just when I think they've reached the limits of the absurd, they come up with something else. How do you read this? What's he up to?"

"I think he's trying to control what gets out. He doesn't want any surprises. Doesn't want anything in the newspapers that hasn't gone through him. I didn't realize the full extent of it until this morning. Actually, I'm not supposed to be doing this—I mean talking to people. I'm sure he would be appalled if he knew I was over here."

"I'll tell you something. It's dangerous to get mixed up with that bunch over there." Durrell points in the general direction of Stockton Tower.

"It was foolish of me, I realize. It was also foolish of me to show you the letter. O'Connor never actually said so, but I don't think he wants this getting around, I mean my part in it. So this is just between the two of us."

"Your secret's safe with me. But if you keep nosing around the English Department, it's going to be hard to keep it quiet."

Cory is not comforted by the vow of secrecy. Durrell appears temperamentally incapable of discretion. "I don't plan to make a habit of it," he says. "I was just talking to Jack—you and he are the only ones who know about this, by the way—and he was very close-mouthed about the department. I got the idea that he and

O'Connor were both anxious to hide something."

"And you figured me for the man who would tell all."

"No, I was just wandering around when I saw your door."

"Well, the truth is I *am* your man. What do you want to know?"

Cory smiles, but he feels a quaver in his voice. "Is it possible that somebody in your department, well, had some connection with Sanders' death?"

"You've used an interesting word there—*connection*. We're *all* connected to the murder in crucial ways, even you. But then we're all connected to each other in crucial ways. Take the two of us. We meet in the hallway by accident, apparently, yet we instantly discover all sorts of connections. I've read something you've written—I even have a reference to you in an essay. You and I are connected through Jack Abbott, and numerous other people. Do you know I've talked to your ex-wife on a number of occasions? An incredible woman, if I may say so."

Cory tries to ignore the last remark. "But about Sanders' death—"

"I'm suggesting that it's not as simple as you make it appear. Connections are very ambiguous and far-reaching."

"Is this another theory of yours?"

"Yes."

"Well, then by your own admission it's wrong."

"Yes, but very interesting. It may even give you some insight into the murder."

"I'm afraid I don't follow you."

"Okay, let's drop it then. The answer to your question is yes."

"Yes what?"

"Yes, it's actually possible that somebody in the department is connected, let us say, in an intimate way with Sanders' death."

"Are you guessing or do you know something?"

"With you and me everything is theoretical, isn't it?"

"You're guessing."

"More or less, but it stands to reason, doesn't it? I mean the nature of the act, the nature of the man. It was apparently an act of great feeling, and almost all the people with the greatest passion toward Sanders are right here."

"What exactly was it about him, if you don't mind saying, that caused people to have such strong feelings about him?"

"Before I answer that could I ask *you* something?"

"Fine."

"What exactly is it we're doing here? I mean, are we just two people gossiping, or am I part of some semi-official investigation?"

"I would say two people talking about what everybody else around here must be talking about today."

"But as the *coordinator*"—he bears down hard on the word— "do you have access to the police reports?"

"Yes."

"So you'll know whatever evidence gets turned up."

"Assuming it gets into the reports."

"This is an intriguing situation, isn't it. You and I have spent most of our adult lives interpreting literary puzzles, proposing sophisticated solutions to arcane problems. And here we have a real honest-to-God puzzle. And not only that, we have two different slants on it. I know the people involved. You have access to the so-called facts. Wouldn't it be interesting . . ." He lets it hang there, looking out his open door into the hallway.

"You mean unofficially, of course," Cory says. "Just as an exercise in theory."

"Of course. Just as an exercise in theory."

"You're assuming there's something rational here. Something that can be solved. It could be just some insane act. I don't know— somebody wandering through the building, some guy on drugs."

"We have to begin with the assumption that the act has some meaning. If it has no meaning, then we don't care about it. That puts it in the same category as a car wreck or prostate cancer."

"There's one other thing."

"What's that?"

"How should I put this? A possible conflict of interest."

"Let me phrase it for you." Durrell walks to the window that faces Stockton Tower in the distance, so that his back is to Cory. "I'm a likely suspect myself. Is that what you're thinking? What if *I* did it?"

"You said yourself you disliked the man intensely, so, yes, that's what I'm thinking."

"In that case, if we're any good we'll find that out, won't we?"

"I suppose so, but according to your own theory any solution we come up with will be wrong."

Durrell turns back from the window and smiles. "But we're not operating solely in theory now. This is not a literary text we're talking about, even if the same rules apply. We're in the real world here. Somebody actually killed the son-of-a-bitch."

"I don't think this is a good idea. I wouldn't want to keep you from your work."

Durrell's look is pained but resigned. "That's a joke. I don't have much work left. They've taken away my courses and given me the surveys. I can teach those in my sleep. They've taken me off all the committees. They've taken away my advisees. And I'm sick of writing criticism. The fact is I've been working on a novel. You might be interested in this. It's about a man who lives in his theories to such an extent that he loses touch with reality. Gives up his friends, domestic life. Spends his time in libraries researching some arcane book."

Cory glances up but Durrell has turned back to the window. He continues, talking over his shoulder. "All I have now is a plot line and a title. The title, I'm ashamed to say, I stole from Jack Abbott. Only interesting thing I've ever heard him say."

"What is your title?"

"*Women in Cars*. Has an odd ring to it, doesn't it?" He walks back to the desk, and Cory has the distinct feeling that he's the butt of some intricate joke.

"How do you like it?" Durrell asks. "The title, I mean."

"I was just thinking about your theory of connections," Cory says. "You may really have something there."

"Everything's connected. It's just a question of how far back you have to go to find the connection. You want some lunch?"

"Fine. But I don't think this other thing is a good idea."

"Let's have some lunch and I'll tell you about the department."

*

The voice is behind him in the hall as they walk to the elevator: "You're not dressed for the remembrance service."

A woman's voice, light, mocking. Cory turns back to see Durrell stopped in front of a partially opened door.

"I'm afraid I can't make it. And who came up with that stupid term? Do we have a funeral director on staff?" Durrell leans into the doorway, his hands on the frame. "You going?" Cory, who has walked a few steps ahead, is unable to see inside.

"That would certainly be the height of hypocrisy," the voice says. "Besides, I don't think I could keep a straight face when our colleagues start talking about what a wonderful person he was— fine upstanding man, pillar of the university community, example for our young people."

"Careful. I'm not alone." Durrell grins and winks at Cory.

"We'll be conspicuous in our absence," the voice says.

"We've always been conspicuous," Durrell says. "I haven't seen you since they found him. What do you think?" He looks sideways at Cory as if to indicate he's staging it for his benefit—a little slice of departmental life. Or perhaps he's warning her: *Don't say too much; there's somebody in the hall.*

"I don't know what to think." Her tone is serious now. Cory has a powerful desire to see what she looks like. "I've never been in a murder before."

"Have the police talked to you yet?"

"No. You?"

"Not yet, but they're sure to be around. You and I may be suspects."

"We were the loyal opposition," she says. "We wouldn't kill the man who offered us that opportunity."

"Certainly not."

"I suppose when Crazy Jack takes over it'll be more of the same," she says. "I don't see that there's going to be any change."

"There's no end to them," Durrell says. "Any theories about motive?" He again looks sideways at Cory, who's feeling self-conscious about his role as eavesdropper. He walks back slowly to join Durrell at the open door.

"Not yet. I'm sure you have one."

"I subscribe to the Big Bang Theory," Durrell says. "I think Sanders finally fucked one wife too many."

The serious voice dissolves into laughter just as Cory gains the door.

"You can see that some elements of the department are not respectful in their attitude toward this little affair," Durrell says. "Jennifer Reed. Robert Cory."

The laughter stops abruptly and they nod to each other without speaking. Durrell, to counter the silence, recites their credentials while they look each other over.

"Cory's the one who did the essay on Hemingway's women I showed you . . ." Jennifer Reed is leaning against the front of her desk. She seems to be holding back enormous energy, which charges even her wild mane of hair. She's big and good-looking in an eccentric sort of way, and a little frightening to Cory, perhaps because he senses something hostile in her eyes. "Jennifer has a book called *The Rape of Literature* . . ." Cory's gaze moves from the boots and the tight jeans to the violet silk blouse. "It's about the treatment of women characters by male writers . . ."

"Charles, your friend is staring at my breasts."

"Come on, Jennifer. The man doesn't get out a lot."

Cory feels himself redden. "I'm sorry. I wasn't aware—"

"You don't have to go into your act, Jennifer. He's the one who did the article I gave you."

"Exactly. I read it—the bitch in Hemingway. His conception of women hasn't gotten much past the nineteenth century."

"I'll walk on to the elevator." Cory nods to her and tries to steady his voice. "Sorry if I offended you. What you say about the article may be true. Maybe you could mark the passages you find offensive." He turns and walks away.

"Oh, God, a *gentleman*. They're the worst. And a *Southern* gentleman."

He's halfway down the hall, and he hears their parting shots as he turns the corner.

"Sometimes, Jennifer, you can be a real ass."

"You almost said bitch, didn't you?"

Durrell catches up with him at the elevator. "Don't take it personally. She treats everybody that way."

"I'm not used to sparring with aggressive women."

"Well, you certainly lost the first round."

Cory forces a smile. "Abbott mentioned that you two had recently been engaged in a little public name-calling. I didn't know you were on such good terms."

"That was a private joke that was misunderstood. Then the student newspaper picked it up. But people like Jennifer and me are always misunderstood. It's enough that we understand each other."

"I could see that you're fond of her."

"She's one of the best people in the department. Her book is first-rate. It's all wrong but fascinating."

"I'd like to read it."

"It would make you furious. She makes everybody furious, so she's dismissed around here as just another misguided woman. If she had any sense she'd get out. But then so would I."

"If she's the head of Women's Studies, why isn't she down there with the other administrators?"

"I rest my case. The Powers That Be don't consider the head of Women's Studies a *real* administrator. But being here with the peons is fine with Jennifer. She doesn't get on with most of the people on three. Not to mention that at the moment the smell's better up here."

"I can see why she doesn't get on with a lot of people. She's got an aggressive attitude and a quick temper, deadly combination for an administrator, I would think."

"I hope you're not making her your chief suspect."

"That would be too good to be true."

Durrell grins. "I told you not to take it personally. Besides, you don't know anything about the department yet. We've got better suspects than Jennifer. Where do you want to eat?"

"I'll let you decide. Why did she call him Crazy Jack?"

"Let's walk over to Jefferson and I will tell you all. *I am Lazarus, come from the dead, come back to tell you all.*"

CHAPTER EIGHT
THE SUSPECT

At his desk for a late lunch, Inspector Battles reflects on his morning's work. After a slow start it had accelerated dramatically—so dramatically that he felt compelled to phone the Chancellor. He also felt it wise to record the conversation, the Chancellor having earned a reputation for shifting his ground when events turned against him.

He rewinds the tape and plays it back while he finishes his sandwich.

"Sir, I have something I thought you'd want to know about. I think we may have something."

"Alright."

"I don't want to put too much stock in it, but it looks like something—"

"Why don't you just tell me about it?"

"I sent Hutchins over to Plants and Grounds this morning to see who the custodian was that took care of the English offices. I thought he might have seen something. Turns out to be a fellow named Arthur Inman."

"He know anything?"

"Well, that's the thing. Inman was on duty the night of the murder. He worked the night shift. He worked that shift up through this past Friday, but that's the last they've seen of him."

"What do you mean?"

"Well, he didn't show up for work on Monday, and they can't locate him. His wife doesn't know where he is. He didn't

come home Monday night."

The tape whirls silently. *"You know, you might pull his personnel file."*

"I did already, and I found something. Inman has a record, two arrests. The first one on a domestic violence charge where he reportedly held a gun to his head, threatening suicide. The second a bar fight. Cut a man with a knife."

"Well." Another silence. *"You may have something."*

"There's something else. Hutchins checked Inman's locker while he was over there. He found these rags—cleaning rags. One of them looks to have bloodstains on it. I'm having it analyzed."

"Bloodstains. That's fine work, Owen. I don't know where—"

"The first physical evidence we've gotten. Of course it may be nothing. But do you think we ought to get in touch with the city people, have Inman picked up?"

"If they turn out to be bloodstains, definitely. Do whatever you need to do."

"Then you don't want me to go through your man?"

"My man?"

"This Cory fellow."

"Oh, no. In this case I think you ought to go directly to the city police. There's no reason to delay it. But that doesn't mean we're changing the procedure. Just in this one instance. Look, I've got a lunch appointment, but let me know something this afternoon. I'll be back around two. Give me a call or if I'm not in ask for James Houghton."

"I'll let you know."

"Owen, that's fine work. Follow it up. But remember, only if they turn out to be bloodstains."

Battles stops the tape.

They *were* bloodstains. A Benzedrine test confirmed it, and he had phoned the city police shortly before noon. Now he opens his notebook and scans the items he has checked as especially promising. The list of initials and phone numbers contains two checked notations. Beside the initials SC he has penciled in *Cynthia Price* and *Connection with Sanders?* with one check mark. Beside JA he has written *Janice Abbott, wife of associate head* and initially awarded two check marks, possibly on the basis of the voice, but then reduced it to one when he realized that the JA could also refer to Jack Abbott, her husband, whose home number Sanders would have had every reason to keep handy.

There's no need to follow up on either until he sees what develops with the custodian. The only task he can find for the afternoon is to talk to Sanders' secretary. He decides to wait until later in the day—just before she gets off work. That will still give him time to write it up for the Chancellor's man Cory.

For the moment he resigns himself to writing up the report of his morning's activities. Sitting at his computer, he reflects on O'Connor's unexpected reaction to his news. He had seemed genuinely pleased with the development. More surprising, he had acted to expedite it—just at the point when Battles was becoming convinced that he was dragging his feet. Perhaps he had been wrong about the Chancellor. He should at least give him the benefit of the doubt. No, it was the *nature* of the development that produced his reaction. A custodian, not a faculty member. No problems. No scandal. No fingerprinting. No interviews with the English professors.

He rewinds a portion of the tape and punches it on.

> "*—whatever you need to do.*"
> "*Then you don't want me to go through your man?*"
> "*My man?*"
> "*This Cory fellow.*"
> "*Oh, no. I this case I think you ought to go directly to the city police. There's no reason to delay it. But that doesn't mean we're changing the procedure. Just in this one instance.*

Look, I've got a lunch appointment—"

He stops it again. *Just in this one instance.* He hadn't been wrong about the Chancellor and he's comforted by that. Better to know what you're dealing with.

Battles reaches across the desk for the tube of lipstick, rolling it around in his palm. Should have had it fingerprinted but Hutchins blew that. He realizes that he's hoping that Inman didn't do it. Too easy. Nothing interesting about that. A hot-headed janitor with a record of violence, maybe drunk, maybe caught stealing, is confronted by a department head working late. Too simple. But that's the way things usually turned out. He sets the lipstick back on the desk, dates the report, and begins to type. *Inspector Hutchins, in an interview with Eunice Willingham, Head of Plants and Grounds, learned the following. Arthur Inman, who has been employed by the University since August, 2009, had responsibility for the English floors on the night of the murder. Inman has a criminal record and he has not reported for work since the discovery of the body. A cleaning rag retrieved from Inman's locker by Hutchins was found to contain bloodstains.*

Battles pauses and looks up from his computer screen. Hutchins in the outer office is in animated conversation with a patrolman named Bryson. He's evidently offering his version of recent events and at one point throws a thumb over his shoulder in Battles' direction and says something both men find hilarious.

Battles returns to his report. *The Knoxville police have issued a warrant for Inman's arrest.*

CHAPTER NINE
THE BLONDE IN THE PARK

They pick up sandwiches and drinks at a deli and walk to the park off Highland, eating their lunch at a picnic table overlooking the tennis courts. Someone has left the morning paper on the table and Cory studies the box scores while they eat.

"You're actually a baseball fan?" Durrell shakes his head.

"Cardinal fan, actually," Cory says. "Since I was a kid." He sees that they beat Pittsburgh on Monday night, building up a big lead early then weathering a late Pirate rally. He looks through the paper for the Sanders story and finds it on the front page of the local news.

Prominent Educator Found Dead in Office

Dr. J. Hollis Sanders, forty-seven, Head of Western Appalachian's Department of English and nationally-known scholar and educator, was found dead in his campus office on Monday morning, according to a university spokesman. Ira Coleman, Director of Safety and Security, said Dr. Sanders may have been dead for several days. His death is being treated as a homicide. Coleman said preliminary indications suggest that Sanders may have surprised an intruder in his office. The campus has experienced a rash of burglaries in the past few months, Coleman said, the thefts being confined mainly to computer equipment in departmental offices.

The body was discovered by Margaret Bains, Sanders' secretary, when she opened the office at 7:30 a.m. following the spring break, during which the offices had been unoccupied.

Dr. Sanders, the author of numerous books and articles on Renaissance literature, was appointed to head the English Department in 2008. In a statement issued by the university, Chancellor Michael J. O'Connor said, "J. Hollis Sanders was a scholar of international reputation. The entire university community is stunned by the loss." No other details of the death were immediately available.

"Have you seen this?" He pushes it across the table to Durrell.

"I read it this morning. Burglary? That's bullshit, but they're keeping a lid on it." He pauses. "Or I should say *you're* keeping a lid on it, since you're now part of this conspiracy." He points to the newspaper. "Is that your work?"

"I guess that was written before I got on board." But seeing it in print has struck a nerve. "What have I gotten myself into? I guess it's too late to pull out now."

"You may be the one to move it to the front page—*Local Man Charged with Obstruction of Justice.*"

"I should never have told you about it."

"Your dirty little secret is safe with me."

They eat in silence and watch the women's doubles match in the near court. One of the women, a blonde, looks familiar to Cory, but he can't remember the connection. There obviously has been a connection at some point, for she gives him a little wave when she changes ends between games.

"I think I know the woman in the blue shirt."

"The blonde? She keeps looking up here."

"I think she's coming over."

The match concluded, she gathers her gear and walks to the high mesh fence that separates them, leaning forward with her palms against the netting. He sees her clearly now. *Cynthia. Cynthia Price.*

"Hello, Robert. I bet you don't remember me."

He gets up quickly. "Yes, of course I do. Cynthia, this is Charles Durrell." He wants to get the name out, proof that he remembers. As they exchange greetings he searches for an occasion when they had met.

"Somebody introduced us a long time ago but I wasn't a blonde in those days. I didn't think you would remember."

"I have to confess I saw you last night in your bathing suit." She looks puzzled. "In the newspaper."

"Oh, yes. With Sally." She smiles up at him and flicks a bead of sweat off her nose.

"I'm a little embarrassed about the photograph. It was maybe just a tad too revealing. Something about the lighting. I'm sure the newspaper is going to get some complaints."

"Oh, you think it was the lighting. I was trying to decide last night what made it so, I don't know, provocative."

"Sally was furious. She said it looked like something out of *Penthouse*." A pause for a sip of water. "She still talks about you, you know. I feel like I know all about you."

He isn't sure how to respond. "So you two are friends?"

"I've got to run," she says, "but I'd love to talk again sometime." She looks up at him and smiles. "You're looking very fit."

They watch her walk across the parking lot, get into a pea-green Mercedes, and drive out onto Highland Avenue.

"*You're looking very fit*? Does this happen to you a lot?" Durrell asks. "I mean, attractive young women coming over to tell you how *fit* you look?"

He shakes his head. "I don't run into many attractive young women. Women have always been something of a mystery to me, to tell you the truth."

"Including your ex-wife?"

"My ex-wife especially."

"You may know there are a lot of stories out there."

"About the breakup? I expect so. But they're probably all wrong. Including the one I told myself at the time."

"And what was that? If it's not too personal a question."

It is, Cory thinks. But for some reason, maybe Durrell's apparent lack of guile, he doesn't mind. "My story to myself was that she left me for another man, which was technically correct, but now after the fact I see that it was probably inevitable. The truth is I wasn't quite prepared to be married to Sally."

"I'm sure you've got a theory about it," Durrell says and grins.

"I read a lot of Freud after the divorce. Freud says I over-idealized her—'the overestimation of the erotic object' is, I believe, his phrase. She was this beautiful creature that I first saw with a bunch of sorority girls."

"You met her while you were in college?"

"*She* was. I was already out, working in one of my father's stores. Anyway, I thought she was the most beautiful thing I'd ever seen. And she was." Cory's voice trails off, and he sits silent on the park bench staring absently ahead as if he has forgotten Durrell's presence. "But after we got married," he says finally, "I discovered that this beautiful creature left the door open when she went to the toilet and left her dirty underwear lying around and drank too much and made scenes in restaurants. I don't know if you understand what I'm saying. I wasn't quite prepared for a real person."

"The only charge I could make against her is her questionable taste in men," Durrell says. "Present company excepted of course."

"Anybody in particular you have in mind?"

Durrell shakes his head, but Cory has the distinct impression that he does have somebody in mind. "She runs with a fast crowd," Durrell says.

"Fast in what way?"

"Fast in the way you come out of the bathroom with white powder on your nose."

"If there was ever an opportunity to over-indulge, Sally would take it," Cory says. "And that's another reason we weren't exactly compatible. I turned out to be more sedentary than she had expected. And she turned out to be more . . . what? Adventurous?" He pauses, looking out over the tennis courts.

"But you seem to know a great deal about my ex-wife."

"Actually, I know more about some of the people she associates with," Durrell says. "But do I detect a note of jealousy there?"

Cory shrugs. "It's possible."

"Could I ask you another personal question?"

"Fire away."

"How does a furniture salesman get interested in writing literary criticism?"

"Ex-furniture salesman," Cory says. "I'm no longer the proprietor of Cory and Son Interiors. The son in the name was my father, by the way, who took over the business from his father and expected me to do the same."

"But you had other ideas."

"It was the source of some contention, the family business versus the academic world, which is what I thought I wanted, and I was serious, even to the extent of becoming a part-time graduate student at one point. But then in the end the money won out. I reasoned to myself that I could still write on my own, and I have, but it's not the same, I think, I mean not being around other writers, not talking to people about what you're working on—you know what I mean."

"I know what you mean, but you've romanticized the university. Most of the people I work with have the sensibilities of tax accountants, and not many of them have written anything as good as your piece on sports fiction."

"Thanks, but I've never gotten over the feeling that I sold out."

"This conversation has taken much too serious a turn," Durrell says. "Let's go back to the point where the attractive young woman in the tiny tennis skirt told you how fit you looked."

"I still don't know what that was all about," Cory says, happy to move to safer ground.

"Maybe it was about her thinking you're wealthy. You *are* wealthy, aren't you? You didn't sell out for peanuts."

"Moderately wealthy."

"Well there you are." Durrell looks at his watch. "Are you finished?"

"I am, but you got me over here under the pretext that you were going to give me the lowdown on the English Department. The only lowdown I've heard so far is my ex-wife's lifestyle."

"The two are not totally unconnected," Durrell says, "but I grant you your point. The trouble is you'll probably find the English Department a little boring. I'm afraid I exaggerated just a bit." He gathers the remains of their lunch and walks over to a garbage can at the end of the picnic table. "You ready to head back?"

"Every mystery has a list of interesting suspects. An English Department murder ought to be very literary." Cory remains seated, curious now, not quite ready to leave it.

"You want *interesting* suspects." Durrell returns to the table, shrugs, and sits back down. "You're not gonna give this up, are you? *Literary*. Let's see, we have only one person in the department that I'm aware of who was ever accused of killing anybody. Actually he's retired but he still comes in. Raymond Wheelwright is in the Renaissance, and it has been said that he's the most boring man in the university, although there's another candidate in physics, I understand. Anyway, several years ago Wheelwright was attending a scholarly meeting in Atlanta, and he was at the bar of the convention hotel talking to some old fellow when the guy just slumped over on the bar and passed out. They got a doctor there, but it was too late. The guy was dead. Wheelwright said it was a heart attack, but our film man Robert McCabe, who likes to tell the story, says Wheelwright bored him to death."

"He's not a suspect, I take it."

"We probably ought to rule him out. Okay, you want literary. What about our novelist, Jason Kimball? A sort of professional southerner--Mississippian. He's absolutely fascinated with crimes of violence, has an antique gun collection, and I think he collects knives too. And he has this rich southern accent that's so thick that sometimes he's unintelligible. Unfortunately for our purposes, he was a good friend of Sanders with absolutely no motive to do him in."

"Not a suspect?"

"No, but very literary."

"Do you have any serious suspects? What about Jennifer Reed?"

"If looks could kill, as they say, but I don't think the feminist movement has resorted to murder."

"Do you actually have any serious candidates?"

"Now you want *serious* candidates. That's a great deal more complicated than interesting or literary. In order to make a convincing case, I'd have to tell you a lot more about the department and our late head. And I distinctly heard you say it wasn't a good idea to get involved in this business." Durrell gets up and throws his jacket over his shoulder.

"Since we understand that we're just killing time," Cory says. "But I need to get something to take notes on."

"Why don't we just record it? I've got a computer setup I use in the linguistics class. I can burn you a CD."

"You sure you want to be permanently on record? What if it fell into the wrong hands?"

"I've got nothing to hide. Let's walk back. There's a little block of time before my next class."

They walk past the tennis courts toward Third Creek, which runs through the middle of the park.

"You know, I was thinking about changing the plot of the novel," Durrell says as they cross the wooden bridge over the creek. "I could make it a kind of English mystery about a department head who's murdered in his office."

"Agatha Christie, with a set of academic suspects."

"The protagonist, the man, you remember, who lives in a purely theoretical world, gets involved in the investigation."

"That seems like a real stretch."

"It could happen. And think of the possibilities."

"A man like that is apt to be a pretty dull character."

"Maybe not as dull as I first conceived him. But I'd like to keep the title. *Women in Cars*. It sounds a little wrong at first, like all good titles. *The Old Man and the Sea*. I mean, if Hemingway had asked you, you'd have to say no, I don't think so. *The Great Gatsby*? Come on. But now they seem perfectly natural. What do you think? I mean about the novel."

"At the moment," Cory says, "I'm more interested in non-fiction."

"You sure you want to hear all this? Once you get into it, it's going to be hard to get out."

"I can't think of a better way to kill time," Cory says. "As long as we understand that this is purely theoretical."

"You'll also have to take into account the possibility that I have a very eccentric view of Sanders and the department."

"I've already considered that," Cory says. "There's a distinct possibility that everything you're going to tell me will be completely self-serving."

CHAPTER TEN
THE MONOLOGUE

Thinking over Durrell's performance as he drives down Kingston Pike in the late afternoon traffic, Cory reconstructs it as a kind of monologue. He had interrupted with questions at first before he discovered that Durrell was going to do it at his own pace and in his own way, so after a few minutes he let him go it alone. What he now remembers chiefly is his artful manner of disclosing his information. The thought had struck him as he listened that perhaps this was a chapter from the novel he was composing as he went along. And even if it hadn't been quite that, it was easiest for Cory to remember it as a set piece, and like a monologue by Browning, say, it also had the quality of being as much about the speaker as about the subject. As Cory threads his way through the traffic, he slips the CD into the stereo and fast-forwards through his opening questions until he comes to the beginning of the monologue proper.

There are a couple of things you have to keep in mind about Sanders. Otherwise you won't be able to understand a lot of what I'm going to tell you—how he could get away with being such a son-of-a-bitch, or how a man so obviously incompetent, possibly insane, could rise to the top of his profession. [Yes, definitely a set piece, Cory is thinking now. Not the first time Durrell has delivered this rant on the evils of J. Hollis Sanders.] *First, he was a completely charming man—I'm serious—the kind of man people gravitate to at cocktail parties. Good looking, dashing even, always dressed like he stepped out of* GQ *or an L. L. Bean catalogue. He was incapable of wrinkling his clothes or losing his cool. I always thought he must have had a maid to wash, iron, and stuff his shirts.* [Cory, in a long line of traffic at the light on Sutherland, thinking, too practiced, even to the extent of working in a little joke.] *It was maddening to get into an argument with him. You knew he was wrong, but you couldn't budge him. He never raised his voice or lost his sympathetic little smile that made you feel like a dunce for yelling and floundering around.*

The secret of his charm, I think, was that he had no feelings for other people and no imagination. Basically, he had so little regard for other people that you couldn't insult him or make him angry. He didn't care what you thought about him because he didn't care about you. It's also what made him capable of such cruelty—the lack of imagination, I mean. He was simply incapable of putting himself in the place of somebody else, and I think that was due primarily to a stunted imagination. His cruelty was almost psychopathic. His favorite device was the public humiliation, exposing one of his colleagues' foibles in front of the faculty. I was his favorite target for that, but he had others. Jennifer came in for a good deal of abuse and, surprisingly, your old friend Jack. As the associate head, Jack got blamed for any administrative screw-ups.

Naturally women were drawn to him, and not just because of the good looks and the charm. I think they recognized instinctively his underlying streak of cruelty. Every woman adores a Fascist, Sylvia Plath says. His detractors called him a womanizer, but that's too weak a term, like calling Hitler a petty tyrant. The man was sexually insatiable. There are stories maybe I'll tell you later, but I want to mention the other thing that made him so hard to get at, and that was his skill in manipulating people, which is what gave him his power.

There's not much real power to be had in a university, as you know, but power is a relative thing. For Sanders, it meant being top man in a fairly small circle at first, re-shaping the department in his own image, eventually, I guess, the university. It was no secret that he saw himself as a future college president. He must have discovered early, maybe in graduate school, that he wasn't as bright as the best of his competition, but he wasn't stupid either. He saw he had something they didn't have, a kind of worldliness that's usually foreign to the poor drudges who become scholars and teachers. If he couldn't be a scholar, he could at least manipulate them. He decided, in other words, that his path of advancement lay in administration—first, department head, then maybe dean, and then on up the ladder.

The way he got to be department head is kind of interesting. He came here about ten years ago as an associate professor with one bad book—his re-worked dissertation—from some little school in the mid-west. The head of the department at that time was a fellow named Aikens, who had a very good reputation as an administrator and a scholar—he's the main reason I came here from Chapel Hill. Aikens was not in the best of health, and Sanders began circulating stories that Aikens might not be up to the job. Aikens' style was benign neglect, but the department was running beautifully, it seemed to me. It was a good department. Anyway, the stories eventually got to the dean, who asked Aikens to step down in favor of an interim head, Fogle, who really was incompetent. Sanders then fanned the fires of a crisis in leadership in the department and finally got himself appointed head even though he was only an associate professor at the time, which was unprecedented in my experience.

He kept a low profile at first after he got to be head. Nobody knew much about him because he hadn't been here all that long. Then a few of us saw that we were in for a rude awakening. It started with a series of conferences he scheduled with everybody on the professorial staff. I remember getting this note in my box from Margaret:"Professor Sanders would like to see you at 2:00 on Thursday afternoon." Something like that. When I went in he was sitting there in his three-piece suit looking very professional. I sat down and he took off his horn-rim glasses and said—I swear to God—"Visibility, Charles." I must have been slightly dazed because I don't think I said anything, so he said it again, very softly and calmly. He never raised his voice. "Visibility, that's what you don't have, Charles. The Yeats book doesn't mean a thing without visibility. You've never taken the trouble to exploit your work. You're content to write your little articles, teach your classes. Do you want to be a schoolteacher all your life?" [Cory, turning into Sequoyah Hills, wonders if a man could remember a conversation word for word after all this time.] Schoolteacher *was his term of derision for people without visibility. Well, he went on like that for close to an hour. "I'm talking about national meetings, Yeats conferences, reading papers, applying for grants, making your presence felt. These people have telephones, Charles, email. Outside this university nobody knows who you are." I reminded him that the book had gotten good reviews—some people must be reading it. "A handful of specialists maybe," he said. "But that's not what I'm talking about. I want to put this department on the map. When people talk about modern poetry, they ought to be talking about Charles Durrell." He paused and smiled. "And if they're not, then we need to be looking around for somebody they are talking about."* [No, he couldn't remember that exactly. Cory turns onto Cherokee. This is not Durrell's account of his department head; it's a short story.] *He was putting me on notice, and a year or so later in one of our little conferences he was not so subtle: "I'm sure you know, Charles, that your days here are numbered." I can still picture him saying that to me, standing about where I understand they found the body. Who would have thought he would be the first to go, in a manner of speaking.*

In that first conference I mentioned in my defense that the university wasn't paying me a hell of a lot for an associate professor with a book, fifteen or twenty articles, and a teaching award. He let me know that the salary was commensurate with my visibility, and that the teaching award didn't mean a thing, since it was based mainly on student evaluations, and students, as we all know, are notoriously poor judges of teaching. That's the kind of statement he could utter with perfect sincerity, as if it were an absolute fact, that would drive you up the wall. My God, if students can't evaluate their teachers, then who the hell can? It's like saying that eaters are notoriously poor judges of food.

The teaching thing might give you another insight into Sanders. He was an incompetent teacher, not because he didn't have the ability but because he didn't take the time to prepare his classes. He just didn't care about it. He knew that teaching doesn't count ultimately in this profession when you're at a certain level. So being the most professional person in the department, he was naturally the poorest teacher. After a time the word got around, so nobody much took his classes. You might think that would have hurt him professionally, but it's just the opposite. The worse teacher you are, the fewer students you have to fool with, the fewer papers to mark, more time for the things that count. Sanders' courses got to be so poorly enrolled that it was said of one of his students that he was truly in a class by himself.

Well, that conference told me a great deal about the coming years of Sanders' reign, but not so much as when I compared notes with other people. I discovered something very interesting. In every case he went for the soft spot. He was completely inconsistent, so you couldn't even respect him as a man with wrong-headed principles. He didn't have any principles. Visibility was my soft spot, but Percy Litz scores high on visibility, so he was confronted with his teaching evaluations. Somebody else, I forget who, was blasted for spending too much time at conferences and not enough writing books. Jennifer was informed that she had the wrong kind of visibility. And so on. Those conferences put everybody on notice that we were in his hands. A department head may not have any real power but he does have a good deal of control over you if he wants to use it—I mean he can actually affect the quality of your life. Most heads choose not to exercise it. Sanders was telling us that he was going to.

And he did. Those who came around to his side got good raises and quick promotions. Those who didn't got out or got buried. Aikens got out. Some of the younger faculty saw the way the wind was blowing and started sending out their vitas. Most of the good people are gone now. One exception is Robert McCabe, the movie man, who disliked Sanders almost as much as I did. He stayed on, but he's got a chair, so he's above the fray. Sanders couldn't touch him. Your friend Abbott jumped on the bandwagon so fast that he became Sanders' fair-haired boy. I, on the other hand, am now the oldest and lowest-salaried associate professor in the department, maybe in the whole college.

I should have gotten out, I guess—there was no question of my coming round to his side—but I didn't. Hell, this was my department as much as his. I'd been here as long. I was a better teacher and a better scholar, and I wasn't going to let the son-of-a-bitch run me out. It took me a while to see how dirty he was willing to play.

I fought him tooth and nail on every issue until I became his special target. I ridiculed him. I put out joke memos over his name. I turned him into a cartoon. I was trying to get the department to see him for the absurdity he really was, but that was a hopeless battle. My only defense, you see, was to become more and more outrageous, because that was the only way I could deal with him. Until finally I became the joke of the department.

You understand that I'm telling you all this after the fact so that it seems very clear now. I didn't know what was happening at the time. It's only been in the last couple of years that I've understood it. To the innocent eye the English Department was running along splendidly under the leadership of a distinguished teacher-scholar who was being hampered in his efforts to guide it out of darkness by an undisciplined crank who persisted in opposing his every move in the most outrageous manner.

And of course the department did keep running along pretty much as always. It takes about ten years to kill a good department. After most of the people I respected left, everybody else fell into line or just kept quiet, so that the vocal opposition dwindled to two or three—Jennifer and me mainly and occasionally McCabe. I opposed him because he was ruining my department. Jennifer opposed him because he was a sexist.

That never bothered me as much as it probably should have. It was the only thing that made him the least bit human—his weakness for women. His instinctive belief was that women existed primarily to give pleasure to men, and that's what inflamed Jennifer. I think he actually made a play for her a couple of times even though she's very open about her sexual orientation. Maybe he thought he could convert her. And it was probably not his unforgivable cruelty or his more or less successful attempt to break everybody to his will that got him killed. He was almost certainly killed because of the one human trait he possessed. But I'm probably romanticizing it.

Here we're on pretty shaky ground, because Sanders' sexual resumè is entirely a product of rumor and gossip. But teachers are great gossips, especially graduate students, who seem to know everything that goes on in a department. And most of my friends are among the graduate students, so I heard all the stories. When you drink with graduate students it all comes out eventually, and some of them disliked him as much as I did. So there was probably a good deal of creative exaggeration involved.

There must have been, because if you believed the stories, Sanders slept with every graduate student in the department *who was the least bit presentable. This is not to mention unfounded rumors involving faculty and faculty wives and a wider swath that included parts of West Knox County. Many of these engagements were supposed to have taken place right in his office on the famed Sanders leather couch.*

Those were the stories you'd hear about him, not stories about his incompetence as a teacher and scholar or his tyranny as a department head. And of course those are the stories that the Chancellor would rather not see surface. That's one of the reason you were brought in—or at least the reason O'Connor devised this crazy scheme to keep the whole thing as quiet as possible.

But there may be another reason you were brought in. You happen to be a friend, or maybe an ex-friend, of two of the people involved, and that could put you in a very compromising position if things start to unravel. I don't know how much O'Connor knows but the rumor is that Sanders' latest—and last—conquest is a lady you have some acquaintance with. I hope it's wrong, but it was reported that Janice Abbott and Sanders were seen driving down Kingston Pike not so long ago at an hour when honest people are in bed. It was also reported that voices were raised some days afterwards in Sanders' office just prior to Jack Abbott storming out. Perhaps the two incidents were unrelated. You want a serious suspect? You saw Jack Abbott today. How would you describe that look in his eyes? The man's teetering on the edge. But maybe it's all wishful thinking on my part. Two birds with one stone, so to speak. Let's leave it at that right now. I've got to get to class.

Cory is sitting in his driveway when Durrell's monologue ends, but he lets the CD run because he wants to see if the microphone picked up the little incident that followed. There is a stretch of silence, then a woman's voice some distance away.

What are you boys up to?

A short seminar on the workings of the department. How long have you been out there?

Long enough. [The voice gets louder as she approaches.] *You know, Charles, I wouldn't be so quick to point a finger at somebody. A stronger case might be made against you.*

As for that, you too. Is that what's bothering you?

What's bothering me is that it's irresponsible. There's going to be a lot of loose talk, and I would think you would be the last person to be making accusations. [A brief pause.] *And just what is your new friend's sudden interest in all of this?*

He was close to Jack and Janice for a while. I'm just trying to fill him in on the facts.

[Cory hears his own voice, faintly, at a distance.] *I can speak for myself. I don't need—*

You seem to be creating more facts than you're filling in. I've heard that rumor about Janice Abbott, and I don't believe a word of it. Janice has better taste than that. It's always the woman in your little narrative, isn't it? Is that thing still running? Turn it off.

He ejects the CD and tosses it onto the passenger seat. Too much going on there. He can't sort it out and decides not to think about it for the moment. Perhaps later in his study with a glass of George Dickel.

CHAPTER ELEVEN
THE WARNING

He retrieves a briefcase from the back seat of the BMW and walks across the lawn to the front steps. When he removes the newspaper from the metal box beside the door—mechanically, without thought, as he does every afternoon—a flock of envelopes flutter down and settle on the steps.

Gathering them up, he notes that only one of the four is stamped. It carries the return address of the Dogwood Arts Association. The other three have no return address. One of them bears only the words *Robert Cory* in ink, the second simply *Robert* in a hand he thinks he recognizes. The third is typed: *Mr. Robert Cory*.

He unlocks the front door and walks to the study, sets the briefcase and the newspaper in his good chair, and keeps walking to the desk. He sits down and lines the letters up on the desk, starting from the left with the letter from the Dogwood Arts Association. The principle of his ordering is least interesting to most interesting.

The letter from the Dogwood Arts Association holds no surprises, but it does lighten his mood momentarily. He looks down at the signature before he reads it: Mrs. Ray Masterson, Dogwood Trails Committee. Mrs. Masterson is his neighbor two houses down Cherokee. They occasionally nod to each other from their front lawns, but have not, in his memory, ever spoken.

> Dear Mr. Cory:
> The Dogwood Arts Festival is almost upon us,

and as chairperson of the Trails Committee it is my responsibility to insure that the scenic trails are at their peak for the thousands of visitors who will tour our city this month.

As you may know, the Cherokee Trail which runs by your home is the featured trail this year, and I am sorry to say that we have had several complaints about your lawn and especially the lot beside your house, which I understand you own. Mowing your lawn and trimming the hedges is an absolute minimum, but we would like to request also that if possible you use outdoor lighting to show off your dogwoods and azaleas. If the adjacent lot is not tidied up soon we will be forced to take additional steps.

A definite threat. Cory folds the letter and replaces it in the envelope. He writes on the outside *Clean Up Lot*, and pushes the envelope to a portion of the desk he has labeled mentally *Things To Do*.

He opens the next in line, an expensive textured stationary with the simple but expressive *Robert Cory* in an unknown but almost certainly feminine hand.

> *Robert,*
> *It was great to see you today. Why don't you call me sometime—588-2173.*
>
> *Cynthia*

A threat and an invitation of a sort. Or a threat and a threatening invitation. He isn't sure how to respond. He reads it again and then folds it and replaces it in the envelope, which he pushes beside the letter from Mrs. Ray Masterson. He's forced to come up with a new category: *Things To Think About Later*.

He opens the *Robert* in the familiar hand, his decision based on the hunch that he knows what's inside this one, making the typed *Mr. Robert Cory* the potentially most interesting because the most mysterious. As it turns out, he's right.

> *Robert,*
> *You're coming to our house for dinner tomorrow night. This is not an invitation, it's an order. If you're not here by 7:30, I will come over there and personally escort you back. No need to call, just come.*
>
> *Janice*

A threat, a threatening invitation, and a combination invitation-threat. He puts it in the zone of *Things To Do.*

The typed *Mr. Robert Cory* is mysteriously light in weight. He tears across the end of the envelope and blows it open. The two sentences have been typed in the margin of a clipping of the newspaper account of Sanders' death, so that he has to turn it sideways to read the message.

> *Let it go. You have no idea what you've gotten yourself into.*

He feels something stirring in the pit of his stomach. He takes a breath, replaces the clipping in the envelope, and sits looking at his name typed on the outside. Then he reaches for the telephone directory, locates the number and dials.

"Yes?" Charles Durrell's greeting seems designed to discourage frivolous callers.

"Charles, this is Robert Cory. I just got something very strange in the mail—well, not in the mail actually. Somebody put it in my box."

"A bomb?"

"Well, it's a clipping from today's paper—the report of Sanders' death—and somebody's typed something on it. Here, let me get it." He reads him the two sentences.

"Interesting."

"I'm not sure interesting quite covers it. Somebody's threatening me."

"Not exactly. It just says you don't know what you're involved in. I wouldn't call that a threat. Maybe a warning. There *is* a distinction between a threat and a warning. A warning may be offered on the friendliest of terms. A threat, on the other hand—"

"What do you think it means?"

"Exactly what it says. Somebody thinks you would be better off if you stopped fooling around with the Sanders thing."

"But why me? I'm just a flunky."

"Maybe you're in a position to see connections other people can't see. That's what I was telling you this afternoon. By the way, the person who sent that may have given away more than he meant to."

"What do you mean?"

"How many people even know that you have something to do with this?"

"Well, you and O'Connor and his assistant Houghton and Abbott—and the police of course."

"Think about it for a minute. O'Connor and Houghton have no reason to warn you off, obviously—just the opposite. Neither do I. So who's left?"

Cory considers it. "How do I know that you don't have a reason? You may have a better reason than anybody else. Jennifer Reed said only a few hours ago that a better case could be made against you than against Jack. I think she may know something you haven't told me."

"Hey, trust me. I didn't write it. I've been in class all afternoon."

"Wouldn't it be crazy for Jack to send it if it's a dead giveaway? Why would he even want to do something like that?"

"But did you *tell* him that this was O'Connor's secret project?

98

Is he *aware* that he's one of the few people to know about it?"

"No, but then I don't even know for sure if it *is* secret. Maybe all kinds of people are in on it."

"But that's not likely, is it? You can read O'Connor as well as I can, and you can bet he's playing it close to the vest. He's not going to advertise your part in this. He's just going to use you if he needs to."

"That's what I'm guessing, but I don't know that for a fact."

"We're dealing here with conjecture, aren't we? The conjecture that best satisfies everything we both know is that your old friend Jack Abbott wrote you a note telling you to drop it. And you said it was typed?"

"That's right."

"Well, that certainly narrows the field, doesn't it? How many people still own typewriters these days? I know for a fact that Jack Abbott does. He wrote it, no question."

Cory can't think of a response. His mind is working over the possibility that Jack Abbott has deposited an ambiguous warning in his mailbox on the same day that his wife posted a dinner invitation. Or perhaps Jack deposited both. Perhaps Janice had asked him to drop the invitation by and he had taken the opportunity . . . "Look, Charles, let's not pursue this right now. I need to think about it some more."

"Fine. And you're right about other people knowing. I'm sure there are other people who know. It's impossible to keep something like this quiet."

"*You* haven't told anybody, have you?"

Durrell pauses for a beat before he replies. "Not exactly."

"What does that mean, not exactly?"

"Well, you know Jennifer came in at the end of our little discussion this afternoon, and she quizzed me about your involvement in it. I came up with a cock-and-bull story which she did not buy, so I had to tell her a little. But you don't have to worry about that."

"So Jennifer Reed knows."

"She knows some, but she's sworn to secrecy, and it's absurd to think that she would send a note like that, if that's what you're thinking."

"She had time to write it and deliver it before I got home."

"Out of the question. Abbott wrote it, I'm convinced of it."

"Well, I'm not. There's no telling how many people know about it. You tell somebody, *she* tells somebody, Abbott tells somebody, O'Connor tells somebody. There may be hundreds of people who know. These things spread like wildfire."

"Face it. Jack Abbott wrote the goddamn note."

"I'm not convinced of it," Cory says.

"You want to have lunch tomorrow? We'll talk about it."

"I don't know," Cory says. "I've got some things to do in the morning." Then he remembers that he's due in his windowless office at ten. He gazes at the envelope that reads *Clean Up Lot.* "I've got to get my lawn mowed, for one thing, and this lot next to my house." His gaze wanders to the note from Cynthia Price, then to Janice Abbott's invitation. Tomorrow will be complicated.

"First things first," Durrell says. "What's a little murder in comparison to a well-kept lawn? You people in Sequoyah Hills certainly have your priorities."

"No, this is something else. I got another threat today— from the Dogwood Arts Association. Definitely a threat and not a warning." He can't quite understand why he draws back from telling Durrell about the Abbotts' dinner invitation. "My neighbor says that if I don't get my yard in shape steps will be taken."

"That's what comes from living among the very rich."

"I'm on the Dogwood Trail, and this lot's so damn big. I'll have to find somebody."

"Well, you know what they say. A policeman's lot is not a happy one."

CHAPTER TWELVE
THE CHANCELLOR'S COUNCIL

"So what are they saying out there?" The Chancellor has assumed his accustomed position, leaning back in his chair, feet on the desk, eying the two men facing him.

Across the desk James Houghton notes yet again O'Connor's tendency to alternate between an all-knowing worldliness and an ivory-tower sense of isolation. He studies the pattern of light on the carpet and wonders why the Chancellor is not sharing the news of the missing custodian. Houghton had learned of it by chance from Ira Coleman in a telephone conversation on another matter.

"Does the Chancellor know about this?" he had asked Coleman, concerned that there appeared to be a glitch in O'Connor's carefully conceived operation. He was told that the Chancellor was the first to be informed, about one o'clock.

"Funny he didn't pass it on." Coleman did not offer an opinion on the subject.

Beside him Vice-Chancellor Edgar Ammons clears his throat. "The most ridiculous thing I heard was from a man over in Chemistry." Ammons leans forward in his chair. "He said it was unthinkable that something like this should happen at a major research institution. Like it was something appropriate only for community colleges. He seemed to be blaming us, as if we had somehow let the standards slip."

"Hell, they always blame us," O'Connor says. "That's the nature of your basic professorial type. It's always administrators who let things like this happen. But I can deal with that. What we need to head off are rumors of a specific nature, if you understand my meaning, rumors with a name attached."

"The man in Chemistry was right in a way," Houghton says, "It *is* unthinkable. Incredible. Beyond belief. People can't quite grasp it. It's something that happens over in the projects, or with drug dealers or criminals, not on a university campus."

"They're just stunned at the moment," O'Connor says, "but pretty soon the rumors will start. Heard anything from the English Department?"

"I made a point of having lunch with Percy Litz," Houghton says. "He's the most notorious gossip in that department."

"What's the word?"

"Well, for one thing, they're a little worried about Jack Abbott. They don't know if he's actually up to this. Not himself, people say. On edge, jittery, indecisive, maybe even a little irrational at times. If you didn't know better, Litz says, you'd think he was somehow involved."

"Jesus. That's exactly what I was concerned about. We can't have that kind of talk."

"People are going to talk," Ammons says. "There's nothing you can do about it."

"I don't know about that," O'Connor says. "I need to have a little chat with Jack Abbott, and a memo to the English faculty might be in order. Loose talk is what we don't need at the moment."

"That may not be your biggest problem," Houghton says.

"I love the way you keep making this my problem."

"Well, you're the one that wanted to bring Robert Cory in. That's gotten a little complicated."

"How so?" The Chancellor frowns. "You met with him this morning, right?"

"Right."

"Did something go wrong? Change his mind?"

"It was a very amiable meeting and he impressed me as a competent man. Smart, articulate. At the time I thought you probably made a good choice."

"There you go again," O'Connor says. "We all agreed on Cory.

What's the complication?"

"According to Percy Litz, a man later identified as Mr. Cory was observed first talking to Jack Abbott, later in the hallway conversing with Charles Durrell and Jennifer Reed. He and Durrell left together, apparently on their way to lunch."

The Chancellor swings his feet down from the desk and sits upright. "That was not part of the plan. I thought I made that clear to him." A pause. "But that doesn't necessarily mean anything. He knows people in that department, saw a chance to renew old friendships. I'm not going to jump to conclusions."

"*Loose cannon* was the term that came to mind," Houghton says.

"Chuck Travis would've been my choice," Ammons says.

The Chancellor ignores him. "I'm going to assume for the moment that Cory was renewing old friendships. If I hear otherwise, I'll give him a call. Who recognized him anyway?"

"Litz said Durrell introduced Cory to Jennifer Reed. It seems she had read something he'd written which she regarded as sexist. At least that's what she told Litz. Called him a Southern gentleman. Apparently in her lexicon that's right up there with sexist pig."

"Interesting that he should have talked to the two people in that department who had the greatest resentment against Sanders."

"I'm sure he got some fascinating stories," Houghton says.

"This is not good," Ammons says.

Hearing the satisfaction in Ammons' voice—*he actually wants this to fall apart*—Houghton is thinking, *Okay, this is his moment to break the news. A suspect. Everything's changed. Maybe it's not as bad as you suppose.* The window beside the Chancellor's desk casts a rectangle of light against the far wall, and Houghton keeps his eyes on the yellow sky behind the glove factory across the river.

The Chancellor leans back in his chair and returns his feet back to the desktop. "All of this may have been rendered moot by what happened today." He pauses for effect. "The people over in Safety and Security have a suspect."

"A serious suspect?" Ammons asks.

"I don't know how serious. A custodian who didn't show up for work yesterday and some bloody cleaning rags. The custodian also happens to be the one who works the English Department floors, and was there the night of the murder. And there are some other things, a criminal record, I believe."

"What does he say, the custodian?" Ammons' tone has changed.

"They haven't found him yet."

"A custodian," Ammons says almost to himself, trying to worry through the implications.

Houghton, who has thought about some of the implications, says, "A custodian, as opposed to, say, somebody on the professorial staff, would be—"

"That would be a fortunate turn of events." The Chancellor has also considered the implications. "No question. That would end all English Department rumors, and we could let Mr. Cory return to his own work. And we could all go back to the work they pay us for."

"Too good to be true," Houghton says.

"Probably," the Chancellor says. "The way our luck's running."

CHAPTER THIRTEEN
THE BLONDE IN THE BEDROOM

After dinner Cory sits in the study and considers the question of coincidence. It's his way of coming at the events of his day from an oblique angle.

He'd scrutinized the box scores, his nightly summer ritual, earlier in the park, and there's nothing he wants to read. An old black and white movie is playing on his television screen but it doesn't engage him. He has drunk two after-dinner whiskeys and is now regretting it, for his mind has slowed to a snail's pace and odd associations are forming. On the screen a butler presents a well-dressed man a letter on a little silver tray. The man lays it aside and pours himself a drink. *Let it go. You have no idea what you've gotten yourself into.*

Cory is thinking about a *New Yorker* piece he read years earlier—something about Mars. The details of the essay have long since disappeared, but one absurd analogy keeps coming back. A scientist, asked about the odds against discovering life on Mars, had countered with a question: what would be the odds of the first bomb falling on Leningrad in the Second World War killing the only elephant in the Leningrad zoo? Incalculable, but that in fact was exactly what happened. The odds meant nothing set against a dead elephant.

Is that the right way to think about coincidence? Probably not. It's like formulating a question after you have the answer, but it's also comforting at the moment.

What were the odds against a particular car from Florida and one from Ohio intersecting abruptly at the West Hills exit of

Interstate 40? Several million to one probably, but they had done just that sometime last night. He has just read an account of it. What were the odds against the *Titanic* meeting an otherwise undistinguished iceberg at a certain point in the Atlantic? And what were the odds that Thomas Hardy would write a poem about it? Incalculable, but it did and he did.

Before the fact, the odds are staggering; afterwards they're a hundred percent. Either the first bomb dropped on Leningrad killed the only elephant in the Leningrad zoo or it did not. Either the *Titanic* hit a particular iceberg in a particular place or it did not..

What were the odds of meeting somebody who is writing a book with a title based on a crazy, throw-away notion you formulated while sitting in your car years ago? Before the event, staggering. Afterwards, the simplest explanation in the world. What were the odds of being drawn into a murder investigation in which the chief suspect turns out to be your former best friend? Incalculable, except . . . If the *reason* you were drawn in was that the chief suspect *was* your former friend, the chances were one in one. And those people with their notes in his mailbox? Three in three if each had a reason. It is only the unknown element that creates the notion of coincidence. An omniscient witness charting the course of the *Titanic* and the iceberg would have seen the event as inevitable. As did Thomas Hardy, for that matter.

Everything that has meaning is ultimately connected with everything else, Durrell had said. But how far back do you have to go to find the connection, or how far into the future? The notion of coincidence is a mental formulation, therefore false. The deceitful mind at work trying to make things interesting. Things have either happened or they haven't. *You have no idea what you've gotten yourself into.* What *have* you gotten yourself into? Is there some connection you're missing? If it's there, if things are connected, you'll eventually discover it. You can't let it go now.

Very well, then, how do you explain the other apparent coincidence that occurred after the first drink. (The well-dressed man on the screen is now reading the letter with a look of pained surprise.) After the first drink he had wandered over to the desk and picked up the note from Cynthia Price. *Why don't you call me sometime—588-2173*. He had looked at it for a moment, then dialed the number.

The voice—the intimately known and remembered voice— had stunned him. *Hello . . . Hello? . . . Are you going to say something or are you going to sit there like an idiot? I hear you breathing.* A breathtakingly level-headed woman's voice, a clear, unmistakably beautiful voice. *I'm going to hang up now and take an Alka-Seltzer Plus. Maybe you can find some other way to amuse yourself.* He had heard the click, replaced the phone carefully and walked back to his chair, where he had poured himself another drink. It was at that point that he had begun to ponder the notion of coincidence, working his way from least interesting to most interesting.

Most interesting. What were the odds against dialing the number of a woman you just met in the park and being greeted by the long absent, long remembered voice of your ex-wife? Put in those terms it's an astounding coincidence, beyond calculation, a great mystery. But put it another way. What were the chances of dialing the number of Sally's friend and having Sally answer? Pretty good, actually. Everything that has meaning is ultimately connected to everything else. If she were not Sally's friend, she would not have approached you in the park or left her number in your mailbox. No mystery there, only the mind's endless attempt to concoct one. *It can never be satisfied, the mind, never.*

And Durrell's account of the English Department—a work of pure imagination. How can you trust a man who's writing a novel about a murdered department head? It was the *novel* Durrell was narrating. Sanders was probably a very ordinary man who was killed because . . . Why? No matter now. It will all come out or it won't.

There are no mysteries, only the absence of facts and the mind's endless effort to fill in the gaps. The last page of the mystery novel is always a disappointment. He looks at his empty glass. One more? No, too much already.

Either Janice Abbott had an affair with Sanders or she didn't. Either Jack Abbott killed his department head or he didn't. The answers are dull; the questions are interesting, but only until they're answered. It's true—you have no idea what you've gotten yourself into. But whoever wrote that note does have an idea. And how does he know what you've gotten yourself into? Or she? A very incriminating note.

He sits in his chair and looks around the room at the books piled on books, the magazines and journals. He locates the remote beside the chair and turns off the television set. Walking over to click off the lamp on the desk he sees the folded newspaper photograph he had sailed across the carpet the night before. He nudges it with his toe until the two women lie before him.

"Goodnight, Sally," he says. "It was good to talk to you."

The sound of the doorbell startles him, and he glances at his watch—after midnight. Only people who want to do you harm ring your doorbell after midnight. He makes his way unsteadily to the front entry, unlocks the door, and eases it open. Cynthia Price smiles up at him.

"The strangest thing just happened," she says. "I'm glad you're still up."

Sober, he would certainly have been astonished by the sight of Cynthia Price at his doorstep. In his present state it seems entirely logical, the result of inevitable forces of cause and effect.

"The iceberg," he says. "Come on in."

"I beg your pardon?"

"Nothing. Just something I was thinking about. Nothing."

"I do believe you've been drinking, Robert."

"Is it that obvious?" He doesn't know quite where to take her, never having entertained in the house before, but she seems perfectly at home. She wanders through the living room, taking in everything while she chats. He notes that she is outfitted for a party.

"Isn't it awful to come barging in so late? It's my car. I was just leaving the Moores and it started acting funny. Do you know the Moores—about five houses down? Then all the little red lights came on, and I thought I'd better get some help. Isn't it the strangest thing? There I was sitting right in front of your house. I mean twice in one day—did you get my note? It's funny how things like that happen. Have you ever noticed it?"

"Yes."

"You see somebody for the first time in years and then you seem to run into them everywhere."

"Coincidence," he says. "Funny thing." She smiles mischievously and he is made aware that *coincidence* is somewhat more difficult to pronounce than he had thought. "I called you earlier this evening," he says. "But you weren't home . . . as you know, of course."

"That was sweet of you. Where does this go?"

"That's the study on the right there."

"This must be where you spend your time."

"Mostly."

"It looks lived in."

"It's a mess, I'm afraid."

"Is this what you've been drinking?"

"Yes. Would you like some?"

"No, thanks. The Moores served champagne cocktails, and I'm afraid I had at least one too many. But have one yourself."

"I've also had one too many, maybe two. Do you think I ought to call somebody?"

"Why?"

"Your car."

"Oh, yes. After you show me through your big house. Where does this go?"

"That's the master bedroom to the left."

"Do you think I might peek in?"

"Well, sure . . ."

"And this must be your bed."

" Well, yes . . . That's it."

She sits on the side of the bed and bounces up and down, as if testing the mattress. "Do you have trouble with your back?"

"No more than most people, I guess."

"This mattress is very soft. When I had trouble with my back, the doctor recommended a firm mattress and it did wonders. Do you mind if I test it?"

"Go ahead."

She lies on her back and looks up at the ceiling. "Much too soft."

"Maybe I'll look into a new mattress."

"It'll do wonders."

"You're probably wrinkling your dress. It's very beautiful, by the way. Your dress."

"Thank you. It's one of my favorites. It has only one drawback."

"What's that?"

"Lean down and I'll tell you." He obeys and she props herself on an elbow to whisper in his ear. "It's so tight around the hips that you can't wear certain undergarments. The lines show." She falls back on the pillow.

"Oh, really? You're not teasing me, are you?"

"I wouldn't dare tease Sally's ex-husband. And of course something like that can be verified." She smiles up at the ceiling.

"Is this something you and Sally cooked up?"

"Oh, no. And please don't ever tell her. She would be jealous of me seeing the house first."

"So it's a competition."

"You look so tired, and here I am in your bed. You want to join me? I can make room."

She does make room, and he decides that it's easiest just to obey her, as he does for almost the remainder of the evening.

It's not quite morning when he goes out with her to inspect the car. It appears to work perfectly. "It must have been those little red lights that confused me," she says, looking up at him from behind the steering wheel. After she drives away, he stands for a long time in the dark, thinking that having no idea of what you've gotten yourself into might not be altogether a bad thing.

110

WEDNESDAY

CHAPTER FOURTEEN
THE BOMBSHELL

"So what have we learned so far?"

Charles Durrell leans back in the booth and contemplates his club sandwich. They are in a restaurant on Jefferson Avenue called The Varsity Inn, a student hang-out. It is a narrow room with a row of booths on each side of an aisle—a bar in front, electronic games in the back. It features beer and sandwiches.

"We?" Sitting across from Durrell, Cory pushes his burger aside. "It's interesting how you've insinuated yourself into a murder investigation."

"You're not going to finish that?"

"Not quite up to it. Rough night—I didn't get much sleep. I think my mattress may be too soft." He gets the waiter's attention. "Could I get a cup of coffee?"

"I was thinking abut this whole thing last night," Durrell says. "It's not quite fair. I've told you everything I know about Sanders and the department, and you haven't told me jack shit."

"I told you about the note."

"I mean the official stuff, the autopsy, cause of death, all the technical stuff from the police reports."

"I never said I was going to disclose the information in the police reports. You just assumed that."

"So you're going to keep it to yourself? Then what the hell are we doing here?"

"Yesterday I didn't think it was a good idea to share the reports. What I learned this morning changes everything. You'll probably be reading about it on the front page tomorrow."

"A bombshell?"

"A small bombshell."

"Would you like to tell me about it?"

"All in good time. And, by the way, your theory about Jack doesn't hold up against the facts in the latest reports. I'm afraid you're going to have to drop him as your chief suspect."

"Ah, yes, the facts, in quotation marks. There are no facts, as Nietzsche informed us, only interpretations."

"Still, there they are, whatever you call them. What do you want to know?"

"Everything they know, or think they know, the police, the Chancellor. And from the beginning, if you don't mind. When was he killed? How was he killed? The facts." Durrell encloses the last word in air quotes.

"Okay. Sanders was killed sometime after six on the Friday evening before the spring break. The murder weapon was a cut glass tennis trophy in combination with Sanders' coffee table, which he may have hit on the way down."

"Margaret told people it was missing, the famous tennis trophy."

"It's not just missing, it was smashed. They found glass in the carpet. They also found cocaine in the carpet. A bottle of scotch and two glasses were on the coffee table. Did you know that?"

"I didn't know that, but I'm not surprised. What else?"

"That's about it from the first reports. They didn't have much to go on."

"Nothing you've told me changes my mind about Jack Abbott. It was clearly an unpremeditated act—the fact that the weapon was something in the office. The scotch, the two glasses—Sanders was going to give him a drink, but they never got to that. They had an argument and it got out of hand. Whammo. He beat the shit out of him with his own tennis trophy. Poetic justice."

"I thought we were dealing with the so-called facts at the moment.."

"Would you deny that Jack has a violent temper? I would

consider that as much a fact as anything you've told me so far."

"Okay, I'll give you that. Jack's a hothead, but it never lasts very long."

"It doesn't take very long."

They pause while the waiter brings the coffee, and sit in silence until he has walked back to the bar. "Remember," Cory says. "You haven't heard today's reports. And you're building this whole theory on a very weak foundation—a rumor about an affair with Janice Abbott. How reliable is the source?"

Durrell shrugs. "Gossip is gossip. But it's not just that. You saw Abbott yesterday. The man is clearly on the brink. Another couple of weeks and they're going to carry him away kicking and screaming."

"His department head has just been murdered. You're carrying your dislike for him a little too far."

"All you have to do is tell me where I go wrong. A mind as keen as yours ought to be able to seize on any fallacy in my argument. Just show me what you got."

"Okay," Cory says, "I've got more than gossip, and I've got a real suspect." He pulls a set of folded yellow sheets from inside his jacket. "Two reports this morning. I'm taking them out of order. We'll proceed from least interesting to most interesting, although everything here is *relatively* interesting." He scans the first page. "First, nothing on the fingerprints. I couldn't tell whether they were unable to identify any or whether they're still working on it. The report didn't make that clear."

"So get on to the good stuff."

"Right." Cory continues down the page. "You'll be interested to know that your name was mentioned."

"Oh?"

"They talked to Jack, asked him among other things if Sanders had any enemies, and Jack, I'm afraid, mentioned your name—a troublemaker named Charles Durrell. They misspelled your name, by the way. Jack told them that Sanders had been trying to get this fellow Durrell, with one l, out of the department for several years.

And there was a woman, a feminist named Jennifer Reed who didn't always play by the rules. Other than these two, Sanders got along well with everybody."

"That son-of-a-bitch. That means they're going to be talking to me. And Jennifer. We're suspects, for Christ's sake."

"I'm not so sure about that now, because of the other thing that happened yesterday." Cory folds the two pages, returns them to his jacket, and unfolds a second set of notes. "Yesterday morning Inspector Hutchins of the campus police interviewed Eunice Willingham, Head of Plants and Grounds. He discovered that a custodian named Arthur Inman was on duty in the Humanities Building on the night Sanders was killed. He was also there this past Friday night. On Monday, the day the body was discovered, he didn't show up for work. Somebody from Plants and Grounds called his house. His wife hadn't seen him since early that morning. He didn't come home Monday night."

"That's nothing. I *know* the man."

"Hutchins examined his locker and discovered some cleaning rags—no, *a* cleaning rag—with blood on it."

"Circumstantial. He's a custodian."

"Inman has a criminal record. He knifed a man once in a fight in a bar."

Durrell falls silent.

"The Knoxville police picked him up in a bar on Magnolia Avenue yesterday afternoon. He's now in custody. Among the articles they took from him at the time of the arrest was a switch-blade knife."

"Is that it?"

"Nope." Cory shuffles to the final sheet. "Inman was drunk at the time of the arrest and didn't make a lot of sense. He *did* say something about hog-killing which they didn't understand. They read him his rights and in the initial questioning he said that he got the blood on his cleaning rag this last Friday night when he wiped up a spot on the floor in the English Office—he didn't go into Sanders' office, he said. But this would be a week after the murder. They asked him how that could be, since the spot would have dried by then, and he couldn't explain it. But he said he was sure it was Friday night because it was the same night he recognized the smell. They asked him why he didn't go into Sanders' office when he recognized the smell, and he had no answer to that either, except that Sanders had told him not to clean his office, just the outside office. He swore he's never even been in Sanders' office. And he said he wasn't on the third floor the previous Friday, the night Sanders was killed. He was in the building, but he didn't clean the third floor that night. They assume he's lying about that and about the blood. They're going to talk to him again today when he's sobered up."

It doesn't sound quite as convincing now spoken aloud as it had earlier when he'd first pieced it together from the drab prose of the police reports. Still, it's more than gossip and ordinary enough for truth. He sips his coffee. "What do you think?"

Durrell's response is slow in coming. He rubs the bridge of his nose with a forefinger and eyes a spot just above Cory's head. "Okay, you got almost nothing there. Inman's story doesn't mean anything because he's not playing with a full deck. I know the man—he cleans my office—and he's barely functional. He gets things mixed up, and we got too many Friday nights here. We got the Friday night of the murder and we got the following Friday night. Maybe he didn't understand what they were asking him. He was drunk, right? Obviously he picked up the blood on the Friday night of the murder. You did say he worked that night, right?"

"Right, but he says he didn't go on the third floor that night, and there wouldn't have been a smell. He remembers the smell."

"So he conflated the two nights. He found the blood on the first Friday, he smelled the odor on the second Friday and they both ran together."

"Why would he lie about not going on the third floor?"

"He's simply confused. His memory's no good. And if he killed Sanders, why would he leave a rag with blood on it in his locker?"

"He wasn't playing with a full deck."

"He's not stupid in *that* way. He just gets things mixed up. Even a child would know better than to keep a bloody rag. He's just dumb enough to stick to a story he knows in his mind is the truth even when it gets him in trouble. But he's confused."

"I'll give you this much. Inman's story is not one designed to support his innocence." Cory folds the notes and puts them back inside his jacket.

"His story doesn't make any sense if he *did* kill Sanders. It makes sense only if he thinks he's telling the truth." Durrell is becoming animated. A couple of students look over and he lowers his voice and leans forward across the table. "If he did kill Sanders, he could just say he picked up the blood on the Friday night before the break when he cleaned the English Office. Since he's *supposed* to clean the English Office, nothing suspicious about that. Obviously he didn't *know* that Sanders was killed on that night and that the blood would have been dry by the second Friday or he wouldn't have given them that story. You follow that?"

"I understand what you're saying."

"Let's say Inman goes into the English Office on the night of the murder, wipes up a spot on the carpet but doesn't notice it's blood. Why should he? He doesn't go into Sanders' office, like he says. He goes back again last Friday night and smells this odor, which he apparently associates with hog-killing, he says. Then he finds out about the murder on Monday and assumes he got the blood on his rag on Friday, when he smelled the odor—a simple association. He also knows he's going to be a suspect because he was in there and because he's got a record, so he's afraid to go in to work on Monday. Simple."

"It's a plausible story anyway." It *is* a plausible story and it will be some time before they discover that it is inaccurate.

"The other thing is the motive," Durrell said. "There's no reason Inman would want to kill Sanders that I can think of. Sanders had no cause to antagonize him—he was good with people like that."

"That doesn't rule out a motive. It just means you don't know what it was."

"You can't underrate the motive. The motive is all, as I'm sure every policeman knows. Motive and temperament—that's why Jack Abbott is still my man."

"You haven't been shaken at all? Admit it, there's some doubt there."

"I'll admit it if you'll admit that the case against Inman is very flimsy."

"Not as strong as I thought at first."

Durrell smiles. "All we've got are two suspects rather than one."

"So where does that leave us?" Cory looks at his watch—a little after one.

"In trouble. Have you considered the consequences of Inman's arrest? The Chancellor's probably dancing through the halls. This is better than anything he could have hoped for. Just an ordinary murder, no scandal, nobody from the state legislature demanding an investigation. He's safe—*if* they charge Inman."

"He *is* the most likely suspect—the evidence they've got—"

"A rag with blood on it from a man whose job is to clean up things and a crazy story? That doesn't mean shit in comparison with the look in Jack Abbott's eyes. Unfortunately, it's the kind of thing a police mentality understands." Durrell pauses, searching for something. "Do you think Arthur Inman sent you that note?"

It's curious. Before lunch he had been positive that Durrell was wrong about Abbott. Physical evidence, a suspect in custody. Now it's fuzzy again, and nothing has changed really except the case against the custodian. Durrell is right about that. And he's right about O'Connor. The case is all circumstantial but it's the Chancellor's salvation. Inman's story *is* crazy. Maybe if they understood it better . . . He makes a mental note: *Things to do. The key is the custodian's story.* He isn't as quick as Durrell. He needs to be sitting in his chair in the study. Maybe after dinner with the Abbotts, if he doesn't drink too much.

"I can tell you more about Jack tomorrow. I'm having dinner with him and Janice tonight."

"You didn't tell me that."

"I just told you, and besides it has nothing to do with the Sanders thing. It's personal."

"You are a very naive fellow," Durrell says. "You don't know why you were invited? He's desperate to find out what you know. Better not tell him you've been talking to me, it'll drive him crazy. I'm the repository of everything he's afraid of leaking out."

"I'll be interested to see if he lives up to your expectations."

"I'd advise you not to tell him anything. Don't tell him about Inman either. Just watch him. By the end of the evening I'll bet you'll be on my side."

"Maybe he's already heard about Inman. O'Connor may have told him."

"You're right. If he's heard, all bets are off."

*

He *has* heard. Cory is sure of that when Jack Abbott greets him at the door a few hours later.

"I see you're as punctual as ever," he says. He's grinning and he looks exactly like a man who has just been told that it's not cancer. "Come on in. The women are upstairs."

"The women?" He hasn't considered the possibility of other guests.

"It wasn't *my* idea," Jack says as they walk into the living room.

"It was my idea." Janice's voice floats down the stairway. "And I think it was a wonderful idea."

Then the other voice. "We were talking just now of summer evenings in Knoxville, Tennessee."

"Hello, Sally," he says.

CHAPTER FIFTEEN
AT THE ABBOTTS'

After dinner they arrange themselves around the coffee table in the living room, he and Sally facing each other in identical wingback chairs, Janice stretched back lazily on the sofa. Jack, whose chair is at the edge of the circle, keeps escaping to bring in coffee, pour more wine, set out after-dinner drinks, settling for a moment only to rise up and scurry out of the room.

"For God's sake, Jack, sit down. You're making us all nervous," Sally says, but he's already out the door.

"Just a minute. I think I left a burner on."

Janice ignores him. At dinner, Cory had been more interested in Janice than in Jack, perhaps because Jack had been completely transparent from the moment he opened the front door, a caricature of a man who has shed a tremendous burden and doesn't quite know what to do with himself. At least that was the way Cory read him. Jack couldn't sit still, and although he chatted and grinned and made the proper responses, he was not really there. Cory had noticed at dinner that Janice avoided looking at her husband or addressing him. It had been odd, the three of them and Jack fluttering around the edges.

But Janice was a different kind of problem. He couldn't read her, and he knew it was because of something that was not there, something he had expected to be there in her face, her voice—something that would betray her. But it was the face and the voice he remembered. She had disarmed him by remaining exactly the same, the creature of his imagination—the same lovely face, the same throaty voice. Halfway through dinner he had concluded that Charles Durrell had wronged her terribly, unforgivably, with his gossip. But then he reflected that he also had wronged her, and all her kind, by failing to see their depth, their incredible depth. *They are not like us. They can smile and chatter and pass the rolls and be a villain. They are deeper and more wonderful than we have imagined.*

Or it may be that he had concentrated on Janice to avoid thinking about Sally. Janice had seated them across from each other at dinner, as now in the wingback chairs. It was as if she were forcing them to look at each other again. *Here is your ex-wife, your ex-husband. We are all together again, except for Jack, whom we will ignore.*

And he couldn't avoid looking at Sally across the dining table, even if he had wanted to. She possessed the kind of high beauty that makes a catch in the breath, a kind that is not natural in an age like this, as some Irish poet said. Remembering lines of poetry had always been a reliable sign that he'd had too much to drink. He blamed it on Jack's second batch of martinis.

Now, sitting in the uncomfortable wingback chair, watching her demonstrate to Janice the two-handed grip her tennis instructor taught her, he thinks of something an English novelist once wrote. *I write books but I am not proud of this any more than anyone is of their nails growing.* She is beautiful but she's no more proud of it than of her nails growing.

"Are you playing any tennis, Robert?" Sally smiles at him across the coffee table. They try to bring him into the conversation whenever they can, but he's no match for them.

"I gave it up."

"What *do* you do? We're all curious."

"Well, I've been doing some writing in the library, although the last few days . . ." He trails off. Odd, he thinks, that there have been only vague references to the J. Hollis Sanders affair, and he's determined not to be the first to open it up.

"You're not seeing anybody?"

"I see people."

"Women. It's an expression. I'm sure you've heard it."

"Oh, no. Not really. Why do you ask?'

"Did you know that you are a very mysterious figure? Women wonder about you and gossip. They think you're rich and that you have a secret, exciting life. They don't realize that you're just as ordinary as the rest of us. Wasn't that your theory—about women in their cars?"

"Yes."

"Well, you're now the male counterpart of women in cars. How do you like that—being part of somebody's fantasy?"

"I just wish you'd tell Jack it was my theory."

"Of course it was yours," Sally says. "Jack never had a theory in his life. But I'm surprised you want to claim it, having come up with it in those more innocent days before the word *sexist* was in common usage."

"That's the second time this week I've been accused of sexism."

"And I'm sure it won't be the last. Where *is* Jack?"

"Maybe he's making dessert."

"We're not having dessert." Janice pours herself another glass of wine. "Just keep drinking. Do you remember all those nights we all got drunk together?"

"They weren't all that great," Sally says.

"I think they were wonderful."

"They *were* wonderful, weren't they?" Cory says this and is astonished that he has said it. Jack's martinis.

"That's because you two were always gazing into each others' eyes," Sally says. "Don't think I didn't notice."

"You never mentioned it," Janice says.

"There are some things you just don't mention."

"It never went beyond the eyes with Robert and me, did it Robert?"

"That was my experience with Robert too," Sally says, and the two of them dissolve into laughter like teenagers. *You cannot fool me with your schoolgirl giggles. You are deep, deep.* He looks over Jack's collection of liquor on the coffee table and pours himself a brandy.

"Help yourself to the brandy." Jack lights again at the edge of the circle. "What are they laughing about?"

"My eyes. They find them tremendously funny."

"*Au contraire.*" Sally holds up her wine glass, as in a toast. "They're your one redeeming feature. Cynthia Price loved them too, by the way. She said she saw you yesterday at Highland Park with Charles Durrell, of all people. I didn't know you and Charles were friends."

Caught.

It's like Sally to blunder into it. Either she doesn't know or she's more devious than he has imagined. "I ran into him in the Humanities Building and he invited me to lunch. He's read some of my stuff." Janice, he notes, maintains her placid expression.

"Charles is a dear man," Janice says. "Jack hates him, but I think he's one of the nicest people in the department—and the most brilliant."

"I don't hate him, but he's not nice and he's certainly not brilliant. If you had to put up with him every day the way I do . . ." Cory hears the edge in his voice when Jack turns to him. "I guess he gave you the lowdown on the department."

"He loves to talk, doesn't he?" *Don't tell him anything.*

"I don't know what he told you, but I'd take it with a grain of salt."

"He told me a little about Sanders."

Sally looks up quickly. "We're not supposed to talk about it."

"I told Sally we weren't going to talk about it tonight," Janice says. "That's all anybody's talked about for the last three days. The phone's been ringing off the hook. I thought we could get away from it just for tonight. Here we are all together again."

"Well, you're losing a golden opportunity," Jack says. "You've got the man here with all the secrets."

"Jack, you promised we wouldn't talk about it."

"What secrets?" Sally asks.

"Robert here has been conducting a little investigation into what we're not supposed to talk about. For the Chancellor, the Chancellor's own little investigation." He manages to make it sound absurd. Maybe he *doesn't* know about Inman.

"My word." Sally feigns a wide-eyed look. "You really *are* mysterious after all."

"You didn't tell me that, Jack." Janice, for the first time, betrays something he's been expecting to see.

"It's supposed to be kept quiet, or so the Chancellor informs me," Jack says, "But I don't see any reason not to talk now that it's about over. Anyway, Sally knew Sanders so I'm sure your secret is safe with her."

You have no idea what you've gotten yourself into. "You knew him?"

Sally nods. "Cynthia introduced us. They used to go out sometimes."

Why shouldn't she know him? There are no mysteries, only the absence of fact. "This thing for the Chancellor is not what you might think," he says finally. "I'm just a flunky. I write up reports for him and correct Inspector Battles' spelling."

"Inspector Battles?"

"Owen Battles, head of the campus police."

"This morning's report must have been very interesting," Jack says.

"Do you know about it?"

"The Chancellor told me just a bit—they have a man in custody."

So he was right—Jack knew about the custodian. He wishes that he had not been right, but he wishes even more that Janice had not leaned forward on the sofa and uttered a quiet little cry, almost a sob. "Oh my God. They've arrested somebody?"

"A custodian," Cory says. Odd—a custodian in custody. He remembers a line of Latin: *Quis custodiet ipsos custodes*? Who shall guard the guards? He had read it in a mystery novel. "His name is Arthur Inman."

"The Chancellor thinks they've got enough to charge him."

Jack looks to him for confirmation. "He didn't say what."

"My God, Jack. Why didn't you *tell* me?"

"I was going to tell you. I just found out myself late this afternoon."

Janice sits shaking her head as if it were all beyond comprehension, and then she begins to cry silently, tears running down her face, which she ignores. He, Cory, can't bear to look at her, so he looks at Sally, who has grown pensive.

"They've probably got enough to charge him," he says. "I don't know how these things work." Sally raises her eyes to him with a look he can't decipher at first. She holds it until it penetrates him. *Have pity on them* is what he reads. *Tell them what you know.*

"Maybe it'll all be over soon," he says, not sure where they're heading.

"Do you know what evidence they have, Robert?" Sally speaks evenly while she holds his eyes. "Do you want to tell us?"

"They've got a cleaning rag with blood on it. They've got a criminal record and a crazy story."

"Thank you."

Janice sighs heavily. "That sounds like a great deal to me."

"Enough," her husband says. "Any idea about the motive?"

"No motive." He pauses. "As yet." Now he's softening everything.

"I'm sure Professor Durrell will be bitterly disappointed." Jack searches his face. "He would like this to be a major scandal for the English Department."

"He's very bitter about the department—that's true. Especially Sanders." *You and Sanders*, he might have said.

"And he has every right to be." Janice is coming back now, and he catches a sigh from Sally, leaning back in her uncomfortable chair. "They've treated him terribly, and Jack is as bad as the rest."

Jack does not respond.

"He's very much obsessed with Sanders." Why hold back now? "The picture he paints of Sanders is very interesting. Womanizer, sexist tyrant, incompetent." Now *he's* asking for confirmation.

"Nonsense. Charles Durrell is a social and academic misfit

who has created havoc in the department for years. He's a joke. Why don't you talk to some other people? Don't just take my word for it. I'll tell you this—if the university operated like a business, he'd have been out of here years ago."

"Thank God the university doesn't operate like a business," Janice says.

Jack forces the manic grin they've all tried to ignore during the evening. "You can see you've touched a sore spot here, Robert. Durrell engenders very strong feelings." It's his way of dismissing the subject. "Speaking of sexism." Jack is looking at Sally, and they follow his gaze. "We all enjoyed your photograph in the paper the other evening."

"Will I ever live that down? That was taken some time ago— before I was wise to the ways of photographers. He must have spent an hour arranging the lights just to highlight my crotch."

No vanity and no shame. Janice is almost able to laugh, and he thinks of the set scene in the gangster movie—the policeman standing by the corpse motioning the crowd away: *The show's over folks. You can go on about your business. It's all over.*

"Did you see it, Robert?"

"Yes, very fetching."

"That's what I do now, you know. I'm a model. They actually pay me money to take my picture."

"I heard that."

"Have you ever posed nude?" Jack flashes his manic smile again, but he appears genuinely interested in the answer.

"What a thing to say, Jack. Nobody's ever asked me to pose nude."

"It's bound to come up."

"I'm a fashion model. They tend to wear clothes."

"All the same . . ."

"What do you think, Robert?" She stares at him without smiling. "I mean, if somebody asked me."

"I'd like to think you would say no, but then you're free to do whatever you like."

"You always were a prude about women, even with all your fantasies. They were always dressed in their cars, weren't they?" Her voice is hard. It appears that *he* is to be the villain for the evening in the face of so many more likely candidates.

She turns to Janice. "Do you know we never had a confrontation in our entire marriage? When anything disagreeable came up, he just walked away from it. Never a cross word. He walked away from everything that threatened to upset his neat little life. He had no real interest in anybody or anything, just his little books and his little essays. He is a very single-minded man."

"You're right," he says. "You're right about everything. It took me a long time to see it."

"You see how he agrees with everything? How can you argue with a man like that?" She stands up and announces that she has had way too much to drink and that she's going up to the bathroom to take an Alka-Seltzer Plus.

"She's more beautiful than ever, isn't she?" Janice watches her disappear up the stairs. "You should have seen her in *Hedda Gabler*. She was marvelous. Did you ever imagine she would turn out to be an actress?"

"Sorry I missed it," Cory says, thinking that he has just caught her in one of her best performances.

"Isn't it wonderful being together again? Jack, could you see if there's any more coffee in the kitchen? I think I've had too much wine myself."

"There's not any more." For the first time he seems reluctant to leave them.

"Would you make some more please? I really do need it."

When they are alone, Cory feels the tension of what she's struggling to say, hoping she doesn't say it.

"Oh, Robert, I've been so worried. You don't know how this evening has helped me. You're good for all of us. You always were. Jack was much better tonight. I know you think he was strange but he's *much* better. You're good for him. These last few days have been a nightmare. You don't know." *I know. I know. Don't tell me any more.* "And Sally too—did you see how she looked at you? I've been wanting to get you two together again for so long now."

"It was a good evening," he says because he can't think of anything else.

"You don't *know.* Jack's been acting so strange that I actually thought—it's crazy I know—but he's not been himself. I know it seems crazy now that they've arrested that man, but I thought— but it doesn't matter what I though now, does it?" *Don't tell me any more.* "Please don't say anything—I know you won't."

"Janice—"

"Isn't it crazy? And I'll never be able—"

"I put some coffee on." He speaks before he enters the room, back much too quickly.

"Thank you, darling. Hasn't this been a wonderful evening?"

"Sally's little white dress by itself would have made it all worthwhile," Jack says.

"I heard that." Sally models for them on the stairway. "I borrowed this from Cynthia—we wear the same size. Isn't that lucky? Do you think it's possible to become addicted to Alka-Seltzer Plus?"

They agree that it's probably not addictive and Sally announces her departure.

"I should go too." Cory looks at his watch—after one. They walk with Janice into the foyer. Jack has disappeared again.

"Are you sure you can drive okay?" Janice pecks Sally on the cheek. "Why don't we let Robert drive you home?"

"Robert is not driving me home, but we appreciate your efforts on our behalf, don't we, Robert?"

"Yes, you've been very kind. Be careful, Sally."

"I will. It was a very nice evening. Much better than those you two remember so fondly. I'll let myself out." She closes the door behind her.

"Do you think she'll be okay?" Janice frowns. "I've been a little worried about her drinking lately. And she's driving Cynthia's Mercedes. I'm sure she's not familiar with it."

"She's fine. It's me you need to worry about." He bends down and kisses her on the cheek. "Say goodnight to Jack for me." Where *is* Jack? Funny how he kept disappearing all night.

A strange evening all round, he muses as he makes his way down the Abbott's front walk. He opens the door of the BMW then takes a quick step backwards when he sees the figure inside.

"It's okay. Get in." Sally is sitting in the passenger seat.

"My God, you scared me. Do you want me to drive you home?"

"No, get in. I want to talk to you. Tell me everything."

"Everything?"

"About Hollis."

Is that what his friends called him—Hollis? He slides behind the wheel, closes the door, and tells her everything he knows about the death of J. Hollis Sanders. He's past knowing the boundary of what can be said and what should be held back. He tells her about the rumors of Janice's involvement with Sanders, and he tells her about Durrell's suspicion of Jack.

When he finishes there's a long silence, and then she asks, "Are they going to charge the custodian?"

"Probably. I don't think he did it, but he may not be able to defend himself. Durrell says he's not all there." He can't keep his eyes off her.

"Then they may never know what actually happened. What are you looking at? Do you think they'll ever know for sure?"

"Maybe not."

"Will you call me if you find out anything? Or even if you don't."

"Yes."

"Here's my number. I actually have these cards." She fumbles in her purse and gives him the card. He recognizes the number, one mystery solved.

"I talked to you last night," he says. "Or you talked to me."

"Was *that* you? Why didn't you say something?"

"I was too stunned when I heard your voice. Cynthia Price gave me the number. I didn't know until this moment that you were sharing a place."

"She's getting a divorce. But what is she doing giving out our number?"

"She left it in my mailbox with a note to call her sometime."

"That bitch. You never know about women do you?"

"No," he says. "You are not like us. You are deeper than we have imagined."

But she isn't listening, looking past him to the lighted windows of the Abbotts' Cape Cod. "What do you think they're saying to each other in there?" she asks absently. "What could they possibly say to each other?"

"She came by later."

"What?"

"Cynthia. She came by late last night. She wanted me to look at her car—all the dash lights came on."

"She came *by*?"

"Then she wanted to see the house."

"You showed her through your *house*?"

"Just the downstairs."

"Okay. You showed it to her, you can show it to me."

"You mean tonight?"

"Why not? I'll follow you. I want you to show me everything you showed her."

"It's a mess. I haven't even made the bed." *And there's that perfume smell.*

"And I'll bet it smells just like Cynthia," she says.

THURSDAY

CHAPTER SIXTEEN
AT THE CITY JAIL

The email is there when he logs on at eight: *The Chancellor has cleared it with Deathridge. Meet Arthur Foulkes at the City Jail at 10.* Battles reads it over and reaches for the telephone. He knows Foulkes from his days with the city and he's never felt easy about him. Not altogether incompetent, but lazy—too much like Hutchins. And always bending the rules.

"Is Art Foulkes around?" As he waits on the phone he looks out his open door. In the outer office Hutchins is perched on one corner of Karen's desk. He's telling her a story or a joke in a low conspiratorial voice, polishing his sunglasses. Hutchins has been hard to live with since he broke the case, as he likes to put it.

"Yeah?"

"Art, this is Owen Battles over at the university. I just got a note from Ira Coleman to meet you at the jail. The janitor."

"Right, about an hour. This is Deathridge's idea." He says it in a manner that indicates that it wasn't his idea. "He thinks maybe you could help us break Inman."

"He won't budge?"

"Not even after we showed him it's impossible. I don't think he's got enough sense to see how bad he's making it for himself. His mind wanders a lot. Sometimes he seems lucid, other times off the wall."

"You don't think he could be telling the truth?"

"No way. There is absolutely no way he could have picked up fresh blood a week later. And he swears he never went into Sanders' office where all the blood was."

"You don't have anything else?"

"We also got traces of blood from his belt and his shoe sole. He claims he tucked the rag in the belt. He can't explain the shoe. It's not conclusive, but hell yes, he did it. I'm beginning to think, though, he doesn't *believe* he did it. A good lawyer could probably get him off on an insanity plea."

"The people in the English Department say he's a little slow."

"Slow don't quite cover it."

"Your report says he was drinking on the night he identified the smell. Maybe that's the reason he's confused."

"Could be. But he's sober now and just as confused."

"If he's as bad as you say, he may never stand trial."

"That's not our problem," Foulkes says. "Our problem is to clear the case by convincing this guy that a confession would be his best route."

"And the way we do that?"

"The way we do that," Foulkes says slowly, Battles hearing the edge in his voice, "is by getting him to see that his story couldn't possibly be true, and maybe letting him know that manslaughter, say killing somebody in a fight, would go down easier than premeditated. Which is what he's facing right now."

"What do you want me to do?"

"Let's say you come over and I tell him you're from the campus police and you've got somebody who saw him coming out of Sanders' office on the Friday night of the murder. Something like that. You're prepared to produce a witness—blah, blah, blah. If we can just get him in the English office on the night of the murder, then we can lead him through it. But I don't know."

"Does he say he wasn't there on the Friday night before the break? His supervisor says he was."

"He says he was in the building but not on the third floor. So maybe your witness can put him on the third floor."

"I'll see you in a few minutes."

*

136

"We've tried to keep him more or less isolated," Foulkes says, leading him through the cellblock. Battles breathes in the familiar smells—urine, moldy concrete block, stopped-up drains. Almost all the cells on the first floor are occupied, and the faces that look out are familiar too—different people, same faces.

"He's up on second," Foulkes says. "I thought we'd talk to him in the cell a while before we take him down. He's been by himself now for two days except for me and Deatherage. Maybe he'll be in a talkative mood."

Battles remembers that Deatherage's rules are that suspects are never to be questioned formally in their cells and that all interviews are to be recorded, but he's in no position to remind Foulkes of the regulations.

At the end of the row of cells they ascend a metal stairway and turn back to an identical block. This one looks empty. "Down at the end," Foulkes says.

Battles catches a glimpse of Inman as they near the end of the block. He's at the back of the cell, turned away from them. He appears to be standing on his bunk looking out the high narrow window. Then Battles sees that his feet are not touching the bunk, which is not under him but to one side, and that his head is cocked strangely, as if he were straining to catch a sound from outside. In the dark cell he had not seen the army-blanket rope stretched from the pipe in the ceiling.

"Shit." Foulkes starts to run. "Crazy son-of-a-bitch." They're in front of the cell now, and smell the defecation.

"Son-of-a-bitch." Foulkes pitches him the keys. "Get him down. I've got to get somebody." Foulkes is running, clattering down the metal stairs.

Battles slips the heavy key into the lock, knowing already that it's too late, that Inman will never be shaken from his crazy story.

CHAPTER SEVENTEEN
THE CHANCELLOR'S SOLUTION

"Is this good or bad?" Edgar Ammons asks.

"Depends on what kind of outcome you want," Houghton says. They sit side by side in front of the Chancellor's desk awaiting his arrival.

"Meaning what?"

"Meaning whether you want the thing over with, or whether you want the Chancellor to keep digging himself deeper into a hole."

"I certainly hope you don't think—"

"Edgar, I don't think anything, except that it's pretty clear that O'Connor's not one of your favorite people, and I can understand why."

"We have different administrative styles," Ammons says, "but I certainly don't wish him ill, and I would never use this tragic event for political gain. Although I'm sure if the situation were reversed. All I'm asking is—what does the apparent suicide of this janitor mean?"

"It probably means whatever O'Connor and the city people want it to mean, and I think we're about to find out." They can hear O'Connor speaking to Judith, his secretary, in the outer office.

"Gentlemen." O'Connor takes his place behind the desk, and Houghton is surprised to see that he is followed by Judith, who takes the chair beside Ammons, a notepad in her lap. "Since we three have served as a kind of unofficial committee on this Sanders business, I thought maybe we ought to have some notes on this meeting, so Judith will keep the minutes."

Suddenly we're a committee and we're going public. Houghton is recalling the late afternoon sessions after the staff had long since departed. *It can only mean that things are going the Chancellor's way for a change. He's trying to wrap this up.*

"First, thank you for coming during your lunch hour. I know how Edgar enjoys his lunch." O'Connor smiles affably. "The facts are these." He leans across the desk to address them. "An employee of the university, a custodian, was arrested as a suspect in the murder of J. Hollis Sanders, head of the Department of English."

What is he doing? Houghton is briefly puzzled, then recognizes that this is all for the official record. As if this were the first time they'd discussed the matter.

"Arthur Inman, the custodian, had not returned to his job on the Monday after the spring recess. The campus police retrieved from his locker a cleaning rag stained with blood. He admitted under questioning that the blood came from the English office, and he admitted also that he was in the building on the night of the murder. His belt and shoe sole contained traces of blood. The police investigation also uncovered a history of violence."

That may be stretching it, Houghton is thinking, *but okay.*

"As I informed you earlier, Inman was discovered dead in his cell in the city jail about ten-thirty this morning by Inspector Battles of the campus police and Detective Arthur Foulkes of the Knoxville Police Department. Judith, that's f-o-u-l-k-e-s. He had hanged himself with strips of blanket knotted together. Inspector Battles had gone to the city jail to aid in the interrogation."

"Inman never actually confessed to the murder?" Ammons interrupts him.

"I would say that he half-confessed." The Chancellor frowns. "He confessed to getting blood stains *in the English Department.* But he apparently could not bring himself to admit the actual deed, although Detective Foulkes believes it was only a matter of time before he admitted his guilt."

"You've spoken to him, Foulkes?" Ammons again.

"This morning I spoke with Detective Foulkes, with Inspector Battles, and with John Deathridge. We have decided that Inman's death puts an end to the investigation. There seems little doubt of his guilt, which his suicide appears to confirm."

And you're home free, Houghton is thinking. *There couldn't have been a better outcome.*

Ammons is shaking his head. "I'm surprised John Deathridge agreed to that."

The Chancellor displays his annoyance. "Why would you be surprised?"

"It seems a very flimsy case to me."

"I thought your training was in economics, not criminal law."

"All the same."

"What would you have us do?"

"At the very least, the case should be left open."

"So that we can have this thing hanging over our heads indefinitely?"

"It's not what's best for *us.*"

"We seem to have a little disagreement here." O"Connor looks at the secretary. "Perhaps the Vice-Chancellor wishes to get his high moral position into the minutes?" Ammons sits silent. "James, would you like to participate in this discussion?"

"I don't have any position on the police investigation," Houghton says. "But just as a practical consideration, what do you want? An official statement of some kind?"

"Yes, and I want you to write it."

"What about this guy Cory?"

"We're relieving Mr. Cory of his duties. Would you mind informing him of that also?"

"And the tone of this statement?"

"As official and boring as you can possibly make it. Say half a page. Anything else on the Sanders business?" He looks at Ammons.

"Just for the record, I don't think this was handled well." Ammons avoids his gaze.

"Be sure you get that in the minutes, Judith. The Vice-Chancellor respectfully disagrees. Okay, second item of business. I met with the Deans yesterday, and, Edgar, you may be interested to know that one of the items on the agenda was you. Have you given any thought to retirement?"

CHAPTER EIGHTEEN
OVERSTEPPING THE BOUNDS

The call from James Houghton comes in the early afternoon. Cory is sitting at a glass-top table on the deck admiring his rehabilitated lawn and eating an egg salad sandwich. He returned home after discovering that no reports had been forwarded to Stockton Tower on Thursday morning. The sound of the telephone in the study interrupts an extended reverie in which he and a woman in a little white dress lie on his unmade bed and talk of murder.

Houghton skips the pleasantries and gives him the news. "The Chancellor wanted me to let you know that we've had a rather dramatic break in the Sanders investigation. The custodian Inman hanged himself in his cell some time last night or early this morning." He pauses for a response, which is not forthcoming, Cory thinking, oddly, that he has not yet taken the time to think through Inman's story.

"The body was discovered about ten-thirty this morning. The Chancellor is inclined to close his part of the investigation and the police are of the same mind. They feel the evidence is overwhelming."

Dead. And he didn't do a thing except clean up the blood. That was his job. He was a custodian. Quis custodiet ipsos custodes? "I think I need to talk to the Chancellor. Do you think that would be possible?"

"I'll have him call you."

The call comes almost immediately. "So, Bob, is there something we need to wrap up?"

142

"I'm not sure Inman did it."

"Oh? Well, we can never be absolutely sure, can we? But that's where the finger points."

"He had no reason to kill Sanders."

"We don't know about that. Sergeant Foulkes believes that Inman was unbalanced. It may have been a senseless act of violence. He had a history of that sort of thing."

A fight in a bar—not a history of violence. It would be convenient for all concerned if it were a senseless act. "I'm not sure he did it" is all he can find to say.

"There's always a certain uneasiness in situations like this." O'Connor adopts his patient voice. "These matters can never have the neat resolution of a detective thriller. But as far as I'm concerned it's over. I have to turn my attention to more important problems—not of course that this was unimportant. I mean more important to the university."

"Do you want me to come over and write up a final report?" Cory knows the answer but he wants O'Connor to say it.

"I don't think that will be necessary. You've done your job well, and we appreciate it. I believe we can just write closed to this whole affair."

Surely he doesn't believe that. "I'm discharged then?" His eye falls on the envelope on the desk addressed to Mr. Robert Cory, and he extracts the note and reads it over again as they talk. *Let it go. You have no idea what you've gotten yourself into.*

"Let's just say that your job has been satisfactorily concluded. And we certainly appreciate the discretion that you've shown and that I'm sure you'll continue to show."

"Chancellor, did anybody know I was working on this?"

"Well, of course the police, and you've talked to James Houghton. The only other person in my office who was involved was Edgar Ammons, the Vice-Chancellor. He knew about it, and the Acting Head of the English Department, Jack Abbott. He called up after you had apparently talked with him, so I had to tell him. I was a little concerned about that at the time. It was not a part of our agreement for you to be actually participating in the investigation directly. That's water under the bridge now, but I thought I made clear the very delicate nature of this situation and its potential damage to the university."

Abbott *did* write that note. There was nobody else who could have. His mind is racing ahead but it's halted abruptly by another realization—he has something to answer for himself. "I assumed that Jack knew about the internal investigation when I talked to him. He *is* the head of the department, and he's an old friend of mine."

"Quite right," O'Connor says, "and that was my reading of the situation also. I respected your discretion and I continue to."

Then you are a very bad judge of character in addition to being a hypocritical bastard. By this time Sally has told Cynthia Price, who has told half of West Knoxville. He feels a churning in his stomach. Inman's death has changed everything, and he has betrayed a confidence. *I should have told Sally to keep it quiet. And what about Charles Durrell? Would he use it for his own purposes? The whole thing may blow up, and it could hurt Jack—and Janice. Maybe he's entirely innocent. And I betrayed him.*

"You can certainly trust me on that," he says. He has to get off and call Sally.

"Fine, Bob. I suppose you'll be continuing your work in the library."

"Yes." Actually, he has lost all interest in his work in the library. "I'll be talking to you." *You bastard. Why did you get me into this?*

He notices that his hand is unsteady when he dials Sally's number. *Why am I in such a panic? Because I've overstepped the bounds, and the whole thing may blow up in my face.*

"Hello."

"Sally, this is Robert. Are you alone?"

"Isn't everyone?"

"I mean is Cynthia there?"

"No. Do you want to talk to her?"

"I just want to make sure she doesn't hear this."

"What is it? Has something happened?"

"The custodian hanged himself in his cell."

"Oh, God. No. And he didn't even do anything—isn't that what you think?"

"It's what I think, but what do I know?"

"What do you think it means?"

"It means that it's over. The police think he was unbalanced, that everything points to him, but I don't know. All it means for sure is that it's over."

"You mean your suspicion of Jack?"

"I mean everything. It's all over. The police will close the investigation. What we were talking about last night is just gossip now. And I don't think we ought to spread it. It would be bad for Jack."

"You don't think I'd say anything about something like that do you? They're my friends."

"Last night I didn't tell you to keep it confidential. It's just that I wouldn't want Cynthia to know what I told you."

"Last night a lot of things happened I wouldn't want Cynthia to know about."

"You mean late last night?"

"I mean in your bedroom."

"Do we need to talk about that?"

"Not at the moment, but later, yes, we do need to talk."

"I guess we both had a little too much to drink."

"Are you suggesting you took advantage of me?"

"I was thinking that it was the other way round."

"I don't think we should blame it on Jack's liquor. Maybe the eyes. Or that huge bed."

"Right." *And we shouldn't completely disregard that little white dress. Or the wonderful smell of women as they lie beside you, wondering aloud if in the right circumstances anyone can be driven to kill.* "You should know that the bed now smells like you."

"I'm pleased. Cynthia's not right for you."

"And you won't say anything to her about what we talked

about?"

"This is so like you. Last night we did amazing acrobatic things in your bedroom, and the morning after all you're concerned about is your little secret investigation." She laughs in a way that Cory cannot interpret. "This is really very funny. *You're* the only one who's spread the story, so far as I know. And you told Charles Durrell, who can't keep *anything* quiet."

"You're right. I've been indiscreet. I told Durrell more than I should have. And he told me probably more than he should have."

"Charles is the source of your rumor about Janice and Hollis?"

"Yes."

"Did Charles tell you anything else? Where did he get his information?"

"Gossip among the graduate students. You know him, don't you? Charles."

"I met him one night at the Abbotts. He drove me home. I think Janice was trying to fix us up. You know how she is—'There's this *wonderful* man in the department I want you to meet.' Poor Janice thinks everybody's wonderful—even Jack, I guess. She may even have thought that Hollis was wonderful."

He wishes above all else she'd stop calling him Hollis. "Did you and Charles, ah, date?"

"Robert, I believe you're jealous."

"It's possible."

"I'm very fond of him. He called me a couple of times after the night at the Abbotts, and I seem to run into him a lot. I guess you could say we're friends. We talk. Actually you come up sometimes in the conversation. He's read some of your pieces, and Janice has told him all about you, with all your theories and your hermit life. He has a theory about *you*, by the way. You're the one person who's succeeded in living entirely in the mind—severed all your connections with people, complete freedom, all that. I told him it was all crap. You were just a man who liked to read books and write essays and didn't want to be bothered with people. Very simple."

"One of the things that's comforting about his suspicion of

Jack is that all his theories are outrageous. Still, I like him."

"He's sweet," she says, "and very naive. He's one of the few men I've gotten into a car with lately who wasn't trying to get me into bed. And I guess I'll have to put you back on that list."

"I believe the visit last night was your idea. Anyway, I think I'm the protagonist of a novel he's writing. A mystery novel about a murdered department head."

"I hope he changes the names."

"I wouldn't be surprised if we didn't all wind up in it."

"Oh, Robert, do you think anybody will ever find out what really happened?"

"I don't know. Probably not. But there's no need to speculate any more. It's over."

"I don't think you want it to be over. I think you were enjoying it."

"You may be right."

"Of course I'm right. I know you, and we need to talk, but you-know-who just came in with our groceries. Can I call you back?"

"I've told you all I know about the Sanders investigation."

"Not about that. That's all over, right?"

*

Durrell is of the same opinion. "Don't tell me—I know. The dumb bastard hanged himself."

"How did you find out?"

"How do you think? Abbott stopped me in the hall a little while ago. And do you know what he said? 'Well, Charles,' he said, 'it looks like we can go back to work now. I'm sure it was all very amusing to you.' He had this goddamn silly grin—he's high as a kite. I think I liked him better when he was down."

"I guess the Chancellor told him."

"Naturally. They'll be thick as thieves now."

"Do you think O'Connor suspected Jack?"

"I have no idea. All I know for sure is that O'Connor finessed it. They actually got away with it."

"You're taking it hard."

"What do you expect? We were really rolling. We could have done it. The man died for no reason."

"I talked to O'Connor. I've been relieved of my responsibilities."

"And I'm sure he warned you to keep it under your hat."

"More or less. Sally knows—I'm afraid I let it slip last night. But that's the reason I called. I'd appreciate it if you wouldn't say anything. I shouldn't have—"

"You talked to Sally?"

"Yes."

"How did she take it?"

"It's hard to tell. She's become an actress. Do you want to hear about the dinner party?"

"Not really."

"So it *is* over?"

"That's right."

"What are you going to do?"

"I'm going to go back to teaching my sophomores and you can go back to whatever it is you do."

"What about the novel?"

"Screw the novel."

"Okay, it's over, but let me ask you one thing that's bothering me the most. Do you think it's possible that this story about Janice and Sanders is a fabrication?"

"I told you it was gossip. Maybe it was embellished a little. *I* didn't make it up. I told you what I heard."

"Maybe Jack *didn't* do it."

"Maybe not."

"Well, maybe I'll see you again. Around the library," Cory says.

"Maybe so."

Cory tries again. "You want to eat lunch sometime?"

"Sure. I'll call you."

"Please don't say anything about the police reports."

"*What* police reports?" He breaks the connection.

148

A day of broken connections. The last day of something—what?—that began on Monday. Cory stands at the desk with the phone in his hand. What? What is it exactly that began on Monday? What is today? Thursday. Four days, but it seems longer.

He walks back through the study to the deck. His sandwich lies waiting on the glass-top table. At least Durrell has his sophomores to go back to. *What the hell am I going to do? Read a book? Study the box scores?*

The phone rings in the study, and he retraces his steps.

"I need to talk to you about a couple of things," Sally says. "Are you up for it?"

"About last night?"

"Not exactly, but it might come into play."

"Fire away."

"Not on the phone. Could we meet somewhere for a drink?"

"When were you thinking?"

"I was thinking today. What are you doing later this afternoon?"

"I was just asking myself that question when you called."

"And what was your answer?"

"I have nothing going on this afternoon." *Or for the foreseeable future, for that matter.* "Did you have some particular place in mind?"

CHAPTER NINETEEN
IN THE LIBRARY

The place Sally had had in mind was an up-scale bar called The Library in a boutique hotel off Market Square. Its decor is an attempt to duplicate somebody's idea of a Victorian study, with stuffed chairs and sofas, strategically placed small tables, and two walls of fake books.

"It's been a while." The waiter places the martinis on the table and smiles down at Sally.

"Hey, Steve. I've been real busy. Too tired to go out drinking after a day under the hot lights."

"I saw your picture in the bikini."

"Like everybody else in town. First thing people say to me these days. This is Robert, by the way. Robert, Steve."

They nod to each other and Cory is aware that his worthiness as Sally's drinking companion is being evaluated.

The evaluation completed, Steve turns back to Sally. "Don't be a stranger." He walks back to the bar.

"So you're a regular."

"Used to be." She takes a healthy swig from her drink, then raises her glass. "I can't think of an appropriate toast, but cheers."

"Cheers." Cory lifts his glass and looks around the room. "Nice place."

"They get the downtown office crowd and the more sophisticated university students. How's your drink."

"The martini is not my drink of choice, but this is quite good."

"The bartender says it's the vermouth. Some exotic label that he orders from a French importer."

"You said there were a couple of things you wanted to talk about."

"You never were much for small talk, were you? Okay, first thing. There's something that's been bothering me for like a decade and I need to say it." She stops, squinting at him from across the table. "And I want us to be completely honest."

"By all means."

"We never talked about it." She takes another large swallow and fishes out the olive. "We never talked about anything, but I'm referring to the time you came back from North Carolina and found me in the car with Guy."

"Guy? Was that his name? I never knew what his name was."

"That's because we never talked about it. You just packed up and left, turned things over to your lawyer, and the first time we've had a civil conversation since that afternoon was last night at Jack and Janice's."

"What was there to talk about? I come home a day early and discover my wife is having an affair with a man whose name I now know is Guy."

"That's what I want to talk about. It wasn't an affair."

"Then what would you call it?"

"It was more like a fling."

"Is there a difference?"

"An affair means you're sleeping with him, and a fling can be more, well, innocent. And to paraphrase our ex-president, I did not have sex with that man."

"As I recall, our ex-president was somewhat equivocal in his definition of sex."

"Okay, since I'm being completely honest, there was petting involved." She pops the olive in her mouth and chews it slowly. "Sometimes heavy," she says, not quite distinctly.

"Petting? I haven't heard that word since I was in college."

"That's because this generation is not familiar with the concept. They meet in a place like this, have a couple of drinks, and go directly to bed. What we knew as petting has become foreplay. It's a different world out there."

"I don't imagine you're a dispassionate observer of that world." He notes that her glass is almost empty and recalls a long-ago discussion—out somewhere with Jack and Janice—on the subject of *sipping* a drink.

"Whatever I've done since you cut me loose is on my own dime. I don't have to explain anything after the divorce." She frowns and starts to say something else but thinks better of it.

"Of course not. You don't have to explain anything."

"But of course anything that happened after the divorce is partly on you."

"How's that?"

"You decided you didn't want to be married to me any more. You're the one that left me on my own, but we're getting sidetracked here. We were talking about me and Guy."

"And about being completely honest."

"Yes."

"So Guy was the only *fling*?" He pronounces the last word as if it were in quotation marks.

"Yes. Okay, there were some other flirtations but they never reached the level of fling." She drains the last of her martini. "And that's the absolute truth."

"I appreciate your honesty," he says, "and I believe you. The fact is that while we were married you saw other men, and I couldn't handle that, no matter the terminology or the degree of consummation."

"I understand. I know you, and all I want is for you to understand my side of the story."

"And what is your side exactly?"

"I did not commit adultery during our marriage." She looks toward the bar, points toward her glass and holds up a finger. "Do you want another one, or maybe you'd like to switch to something else?"

"I'm still nursing this one," he says. "And with all these distinctions you're making I probably ought to keep a clear head.

There's one jump in your argument I didn't quite understand—that I'm responsible for what you did after the divorce. The problem with that is we both agreed on the divorce."

"Through our lawyers," she says. "We didn't agree in person."

"Another fine distinction, but never mind that. My memory is that you were not averse to our break up. Remember, we're being honest."

"Okay. At the time I thought we probably shouldn't be married any more. I was wrong, and I would not have initiated the divorce. I wanted to talk about it. You didn't." She waves to someone across the room. "Eric," she says. "I've never seen that blonde before, but I've been away from the bar scene for a while." She turns back to Cory. "You ever had second thoughts about it?"

"I've thought about it a good deal," he says. "What I think is that we weren't cut out to be married to each other, but then, since we're being honest, I have to say that I never got completely over you."

"How sweet," she says. "You see how good it is just to talk things out? I thought I *had* gotten completely over you until last night."

"You want to talk about that?"

"Probably better to leave it alone for a while, but last night leads me to the second point." She pauses while Steve, as if aware that weighty matters are at issue, discretely places a fresh drink before her and retreats to the bar.

Cory raises his glass to her. "I'm trying to imagine what the second point could possibly be after we worked out the first point so well."

"Okay, it follows from the first one. We do have a history. We shouldn't be married to each other, but there's no reason we couldn't *see* each other."

"See each other." He repeats the phrase as if not quite taking it in.

"Go out."

"Have dates?"

"Kids have dates. We're adults."

"You mean, say, for drinks like this."

"For drinks, for dinner, for just talking." She leans across the table so that her head is at his shoulder and whispers, "For having sex on your big bed." And then in a normal voice over his shoulder, "Hey, Jimmy."

"Long time no see," says the voice behind him.

"I've been real busy," she says. "This is Robert, a ghost from the past." She straightens and leans back in her chair. "You caught us in a delicate moment. We were just wondering if it's possible to pick up the pieces after such a long time."

Is that what we're doing? Cory turns to extend a hand to the smiling man leaning over his chair. *Not quite, but then what exactly* are *we doing?*

FRIDAY

CHAPTER TWENTY
THE CLEANING RAG

In his dream they are back at the little apartment on Whitlow. Sally is chiding him for being away so much, and somewhere a telephone is ringing. He wakes, swings his feet to the floor, and pursues the insistent ringing into the study. He picks up the phone, then leans against the desk, trying to fathom what Durrell has just said.

"It's not quite over" is what he said.

"What time is it? It's still dark outside."

"I couldn't sleep," Durrell says. "I read something last night I couldn't get out of my mind. I've got it all worked out—we've been asking the wrong question."

"The wrong question. So what's the right question?"

"Not now. It's too complicated to do on the phone," Durrell says. "You'll have to come over here—to my apartment—this afternoon. Stay away from the English Department."

"What do you mean? Have you found out something?"

"I've discovered the *method* for finding out something, which is just as good, maybe better."

Nothing. Only a new theory that will prove as fallible as all the old theories. "Charles, we could get people in trouble if we start nosing around now. Everybody else thinks the whole affair is over."

"This is just for you and me. Nobody else has to know unless you want to tell them. I'll leave that up to you."

Cory sits down at the desk and clicks on the lamp. "I don't know what to say because I don't know what you're proposing."

"Do you have yesterday's paper?"

"I think so." He locates it on the floor beside his chair.

"Look at the first page of local news—the article on something called MEDICO."

Cory locates the article under a headline that reads "MEDICO, Medical Records Program, Launched." Under that in smaller type: "Knoxville One of a Select Group of U.S. Cities Granted Federal Funds." The article describes a pilot program in which the city's medical records from hospitals, clinics, doctors' offices have been pooled and computerized to be made instantly accessible, relieving the medical community of the more time-consuming methods of transferring patients' records. In an interview one of the company's officials notes that the speed of retrieving critical data will no doubt save lives, and, anticipating possible fears, he gives assurance that the records will be kept strictly confidential, available only to authorized personnel.

"Okay, I read it. The medical records for the whole city have been computerized. So what? I'm afraid I don't see the connection."

"I've got a friend in computer science who helped design the program," Durrell says. "Worked on security, as a matter of fact."

"Good for him. I still don't see the point."

"The point is that he would know how to bypass the system that he helped set up."

"If I ever need clandestine medical records I'll call you. Otherwise—"

"I'll explain it this afternoon, but there's something I need you to do. We need the blood type on the cleaning rag."

"We need *what*?"

"You remember the cleaning rag? That was the strongest piece of evidence against Inman. We need the blood type on the rag."

"Why do we need that?"

"Isn't it obvious?"

"No, I'm afraid not. Inman admitted it was Sanders' blood."

"There's our problem. He *didn't* admit that. He admitted that he got the blood in the English office, which is not the same thing."

"So you want to see if it's Sanders' blood."

"Exactly. And I'm assuming Sanders' blood type was in the police reports."

"It's type AB, as I recall, and if the blood on the rag is not AB, this would in some way exonerate Inman?"

"That's part of it, but there's more."

"I hope your theory doesn't depend on that cleaning rag. There was no mention of the blood type on the rag in the reports, and I don't know how I could possibly get it."

"You were conducting the university's internal investigation, for Christ's sake. Call Battles. Call the Knoxville police."

"I've been discharged, remember?"

"Maybe they don't know that. Use your imagination. Lie."

"You seem to have recovered from yesterday's depression."

"It comes and goes. Look, I'm doing all the hard stuff. All I want from you is one small thing. Are you going to do it or not? What the hell else do you have to do?"

"I'll try," he says, "but I'm not promising anything."

"Come over to my place about five. Do you have a pen there?" He gives Cory the directions to his apartment on Clinch, and Cory writes them down on the back of the envelope addressed *Mr. Robert Cory*.

"What if I can't get the blood type on the rag?"

"Then we'll think of something else. There's got to be a way to get it, but come even if you can't. I'm going to show you something very interesting. I worked it all out last night."

"This is just another theory, right? You haven't actually learned anything new. There are no new *facts* here."

"Correct. It's a theory, and what scares me a little is I can't find anything wrong with it. I've got to call my computer guy now. Just do your job and we're in business." And he's gone.

Right. I'm going to obtain a piece of evidence from the police. No problem. He takes a shower and gets dressed, thinking something will occur to him if he stops concentrating on it. Nothing does, and his mind keeps drifting back to the previous afternoon. After they left the bar he asked Sally if she wanted something to eat.

"Let's not push it," she said. "We've had a real breakthrough, but we shouldn't take it too fast. Call me if you hear from the Chancellor again, or call me even if you don't, now that we're talking to each other again. Promise you'll call me?"

"I will," he said and watched her walk across Market Square to the parking garage.

A breakthrough? He muses on the term as he makes coffee, then sits at the kitchen table listening to NPR. In the local segment the newscaster reports the suicide by hanging of Arthur Inman, 47, custodial worker at the university. Inman's death, the newscaster says, marks the end of the investigation into the murder of Dr. J. Hollis Sanders, head of the university's English Department and internationally known scholar and teacher. It is the city's first homicide investigation, he reports, in which the Knoxville force worked in partnership with the campus police. At a news conference Knoxville Police Chief John Deathridge said that much of the credit for breaking the case should go to Inspector Roy Hutchins of Campus Safety and Security.

Inspector Battles is the most likely source of information, Cory decides. It's possible that the Chancellor hasn't yet told him that his coordinator has been relieved of his responsibilities. He works out an almost plausible story and at a quarter to nine dials Battles at Safety and Security. The receptionist puts him on hold and he rehearses his story, which pours out implausibly when Battles finally comes on.

"It's good to talk to you finally," Cory begins. "I've been reading your reports. I wanted to congratulate you on your fine work." *Sounds hokey as hell.* " It looks like it's all over."

"Looks that way." Battles sounds wary. *He's not buying it.*

"There's one detail that I didn't get for my report to the Chancellor, the blood type on the cleaning rag. Did you have that tested?"

"We didn't order a DNA test."

"No, I mean just the blood type."

Battles is silent for a moment. "Blood type?" It's as if he's never

160

heard of the concept. "It wasn't tested for an ABO typing," he says finally. "We had it scheduled, but after Inman's suicide there was no point. Inman admitted that he got the blood in the English Office. Maybe you didn't know that."

"Right." Cory is feeling desperate. "Do you still have the cleaning rag? There's certainly no harm in running the test, is there? Tie everything together?"

"I've got it."

"It would make my report—" He stops. It's impossible for him to lie with any conviction. "Mr. Battles, let me give it to you straight." He starts again. "There *is* no report—the Chancellor relieved me of my assignment yesterday—but I'm not absolutely convinced that Inman killed Sanders. I've had a part in this, and to satisfy my own mind I'd like to see a test of the blood type on that cleaning rag. Is that possible?"

Silence on the other end, and he knows he has ruined whatever slim chance he started with. Durrell is going to be unhappy. When Battles finally comes back, he says simply, "I believe I can get that for you."

"I appreciate it." He's astonished. It goes against human nature and all reason. "The other problem is I need it this afternoon. Is that unreasonable?" *Maybe the trick is to be unreasonable.*

"I think I can arrange it," Battles says.

"I'll pick it up at your office. About four?"

"I believe we can have it back by then. Do you mind if I put yesterday's date on the report?"

*

That was very curious, the Inspector thinks as he replaces the phone. Why did Cory lie? And then why did he stop lying? Battles had of course known he was lying—the Chancellor had told him on Thursday afternoon that no more reports were to be forwarded to Cory. Any future communications on the matter were to be directed to the Knoxville police.

And why should Cory lie for such a trivial piece of information—evidence that was not even in question. Inman had freely admitted that the blood came from the English Office. The only matter of dispute was when. A greater mystery still—why had he gone along with Cory's request? He opens the right-hand bottom drawer, removes a large manila envelope and pours out the rag and a tube of lipstick onto the desk. It would be interesting if it turned out that Inman didn't kill him. If Hutchins' credit for breaking the case was somewhat premature.

He consults his notebook and dials a number. "Yes, Owen Battles. Can you run an ABO grouping for me this afternoon? I need it in a hurry—say 3:00 . . . No, dried . . . Thanks, I'll send somebody over with it."

Battles replaces the receiver and sits at his desk staring at the cleaning rag and the tube of lipstick. Be interesting if this Cory knows something.

*

Durrell's apartment is not what he had expected, not that he knows exactly what he expected—something artsy maybe, graduate student decor with satirical posters and snobbishly shabby furniture. It is in fact a neatly furnished middle-class apartment, quite ordinary actually.

"Did you get it?"

Cory pulls the envelope from inside his jacket and offers it to Durrell.

"That's it?" Durrell makes no move to take it.

"You asked me to get it and I got it."

"How did you manage it, if I may ask?"

"It was a stroke of genius. I told the truth. I called Battles and told him what I wanted. He had the test run this afternoon and I picked it up from his secretary on the way over here. You want it?"

"Do you know what that means?" Durrell takes the envelope without looking at it. He walks back to the small kitchen then retraces his steps and hands it back to Cory. "It means we've got the whole thing worked out. We've got everything we need right here. I didn't think you'd be able to get it, to tell you the truth."

"So what do we do with it?"

"With just a little luck from the law of averages, I'll be able to tell you who killed Sanders in, say, twenty minutes."

"How come it takes so long?"

"It's a little complicated. By the way, have you looked at it?"

"I thought I'd give you the honor. It's your theory."

"Good. We'll find out together."

"You don't know yourself?"

"Not by my *method*. That's the great part. We'll find out together." Durrell perches on the edge of the sofa. "You're about to see the point at which theory crosses over into the real world."

Cory glances around the living room, then sits down in a recliner and sticks Battles' envelope back inside his jacket.

"It's a little lesson in methodology," Durrell says, leaning forward on the sofa. "And it's not mine—only the application. It came to me last night. Why don't you take off your jacket and relax. You want something to drink? A beer?"

"Nothing."

"Some coffee?"

"No. Nothing. Why don't you just tell me your theory? I'm going to lean back in your recliner and listen. I promise not to interrupt."

Durrell insists on starting from the beginning. Last night when he went to bed, he says, he looked through the newspaper, noting, among other things, an article on the opening of MEDICO. Then he picked up a book lying on the bedside table, something to put himself to sleep. It happened to be a book from a philosophy class he had taken in graduate school. "This one on the coffee table."

Cory leans forward and examines the book. Its author is unfamiliar to him.

"That's not important," Durrell says. "What *is* important is a concept introduced in the first chapter. It's not the *answers* philosophers give us that are important but the *questions* they ask. You with me so far?"

Cory nods.

"Early Greek philosophers asked questions about the nature of the universe. Then Socrates came along and asked a new set of questions—not which of these answers is true but what *is* truth? What *is* knowledge? His *questions*, not his answers, began a new era of philosophy. And so on through the history of philosophy. Somebody stops trying to answer the old questions and asks a new one."

"I understand the principle," Cory says. "I just don't see how it applies to a bloody cleaning rag."

"Same principle. We have a specific problem here, a crazy story from a custodian, and nothing is making any particular sense. So maybe what we need is not a new answer but a new question."

"And the old question was?"

"Why is Inman giving us this crazy story? Every question contains hidden assumptions—did I mention that?—and the assumption contained in this question is that the custodian's story must be false, and why is he saying what couldn't possibly be true? The police answer was *because he's guilty and he's lying.* My answer was *because he's confused, not playing with a full deck.* Both answers were prompted by the hidden assumption contained in the question—he's not telling the truth. So what we need is a new question."

"Which would be?"

"What circumstances led to Inman wiping up fresh blood in the English Office a week *after* the murder? This question contains a different assumption. His story is true. There *was* fresh blood in the English Office on the following Friday night. And once you get over *that* hurdle, and it's a big one, the answer is so simple that any child could give it to you. Obviously it was somebody *else's* blood. Not Sanders'. If it was so obvious, why didn't we think of it? Because we were limited by the assumption contained in the question we were asking. Inman had to be wrong."

164

Cory nods, beginning to see where all this is heading.

"The next question follows logically. Who could have left fresh blood in the English Office a week after the murder? The answer to that is also obvious—the person who killed Sanders. Why would it be the killer? Because of two things. First, there was no reason for anybody else to be there. Second, the smell. An innocent person—especially somebody of average intelligence—would have recognized the smell and reported it. One is led to the conclusion that whoever was at the scene of the crime a week after the murder did not wish it known. Do you follow me so far?"

"Yes, but Inman was there. He admitted to being there."

"Just hold your objections for the end. You see, this particular theory has what none of the others have had. It's susceptible to proof, up to a point. It is, at least, since you got the blood type off the cleaning rag." He pauses. "You see how that illustrates the idea of being limited by one's assumptions? The police were slow in getting the blood type off the rag because Inman *admitted* he got it in the English Office. They just assumed it was Sanders' blood. They would have tested it eventually if things hadn't ended so abruptly, but it didn't seem crucial to them."

"You're right about that, at least," Cory says. "Battles told me—"

"But of course it *is* crucial, although with the advent of DNA testing I guess blood types seem too low-tech to criminologists these days, out of fashion. Anyway, we have Sanders' blood type from the autopsy report, and it's type AB, you informed me this morning. It happens that of the four major groups, AB is the rarest—I was on line this morning, amazing the stuff you can get on line. Do you know anything about blood types?"

Cory shakes his head, and Durrell tells him what he has learned—five percent of people in the United States have type AB blood, while thirty-nine percent have type A, twelve percent have type B and forty-four percent have type O. "There are also positives and negatives but that complicates things, and we'll use those only if we have to."

"So you have—"

Durrell holds up to hand to interrupt. "I'm sure you've anticipated my point by now. It's the simplest thing in the world. If the blood on that rag is any type other than AB, then the argument I've been pursuing is right. Inman was neither lying nor confused. He was telling the truth, and the blood he picked up on Friday night belonged to somebody else, almost certainly the person who killed Sanders."

But the reverse is not necessarily true, he explains. If the blood on the rag *is* AB, it doesn't *prove* anything. It could mean that it was Sanders' blood and that Inman was lying or confused about when he got it—the official theory—or it could mean that it was somebody else's blood that happened to be of the same type. It could support Inman's innocence but not prove his guilt.

"But since only a little less than five percent of the population have type AB blood," Durrell says, "the chances are less than one in twenty that somebody else's blood would happen to be of the same type. So if it *is* AB, I'll be willing to say that I was wrong and we'll drop the whole thing. In that case the odds are that Inman's story was wrong—for whatever reason. Then it *is* all over."

"So let's see if you're right." Cory takes the envelope from his jacket and flips it across toward Durrell. It lands on the glass coffee table beside the philosophy book. Durrell ignores it.

"Not yet. That was only the first stage. The second stage is much more interesting—at least I find it so. The first stage deals with innocence—the second deals with guilt."

CHAPTER TWENTY-ONE
THE BLOOD TEST

"I think I will have a drink after all." Cory walks back to the kitchen that is separated from the living room by a waist-high counter. "Do you have any whiskey? It looks like this may take a little time."

"In the corner cabinet. What do you think?"

"I think you're enjoying it too much."

"Didn't you find it interesting? I thought it was good—like the last chapter of a mystery novel."

"The last chapters of mystery novels are always a disappointment," Cory says. He searches the cabinet for a glass. "Too much exposition. Why don't we just open the damn envelope and see if you're right? How long are you prepared to keep this up?"

"We haven't even gotten to the interesting part."

Standing at the counter, he sees Durrell reach for the book on the coffee table and take out several index cards. He looks at them briefly and arranges them in a row on the table, returning the rest of the cards to the book.

"What are those?"

"Those, sir, are the blood types of our suspects."

"I would think that would be hard information to come by."

"You might think so, except for my friend in computer science who enjoys the challenge of retrieving bits of information he's not supposed to have access to. For example, did you know that Arthur Inman regularly sold blood to an organization called Knox Plasma? It's amazing the kind of things you can get off a computer if you know what you're doing."

"So your friend is a hacker."

"He dislikes the term. He prefers to think of it as a superior form of computer game."

"Are you telling me he actually—?"

"Hey, this is not rocket science. And the fact is my acquaintance was somewhat disappointed in being insufficiently challenged, since he knew the system inside out. Too easy, he said. I told him next time I'd give him something harder, like the Knoxville Police Department."

"So he got everything you needed?"

"Not everything. It wasn't perfect, as you might expect. I added some more names just to make things interesting, and one of those didn't turn up. But they were not *serious* suspects. I got the ones I had to have, and four out of five ain't bad."

"This is illegal, right? This information you've gotten."

"Let's put it this way. It couldn't be used in a court of law. But then we're not a court of law. Just two clever fellows trying to solve a little puzzle."

Cory walks back to the sofa with a bottle of Irish whiskey and two glasses. The index cards are lined up on the coffee table. "Jack and the custodian. Who else?"

"I added one last night after my epiphany. I guess I'll have a touch of that myself."

Cory pours the whiskey and hands a glass to Durrell. "I think I can guess."

"I was forced to it by the purest of logic. After my breakthrough last night I began reexamining all our assumptions. One in particular proved quite interesting. Why don't you sit down?"

"I suppose there's no way to speed you through this."

"Just relax and enjoy it."

"We're talking about real people here."

"Enjoy the methodology, the technique of the solution, the inevitability of the mind's reasoning as it unfolds. A solution to a complicated problem has a certain elegance, as mathematicians say. We can worry about the people later."

"Just remember these are people we know."

"As I was saying." Durrell places his glass on the coffee table and leans back on the sofa, ruffling the pages of the philosophy text with his thumb. "We have to reexamine all our previous assumptions about everything. Jack Abbott, for example. Why is Jack our chief suspect?"

"*Your* chief suspect," Cory says. "The way he's been acting mainly. And the note in my mailbox."

"Right. And two other points—his easy access to the murder scene and his motive, his wife's rumored affair with the victim."

Cory swirls the whiskey in his glass and studies a watercolor on the far wall.

"The question is," Durrell says, "can we come up with an equally viable hypothesis that's consistent with these facts or assumptions? The answer is yes, as I discovered last night. What if Jack Abbott suspected, or knew, that Janice was connected with Sanders' death in some way? Either she killed him or, say, was indirectly involved on account of the affair. Wouldn't the same results follow? That is, wouldn't he exhibit nervous behavior? Might he not send you that warning note? The note fits the new hypothesis especially well. It strikes me that a man would be more likely to send a note like that to protect his wife than to protect himself. 'Let it go. You have no idea what you've gotten yourself into.' You have no idea of what? That his wife—your friend—was involved somehow in this dirty little affair. And that you, because you knew her and were nosing around, might make connections that a policeman wouldn't make. He has a better chance of keeping her involvement secret if he can scare you off."

"I can see that," Cory says. He's back at the dinner with the Abbotts, remembering Jack's skittish behavior, Janice's face, the way she avoided looking at him. "She thought Jack was the one involved. At least that's what I picked up the other night."

"All the same, the affair gives her the other two attributes that led us to suspect her husband—access to Sanders' office and a motive. I don't know what the motive could have been exactly, but I do know that in homicide investigations husbands, wives, and lovers are immediately the chief suspects. There seems to be a curious paradox in murder cases. The more intimately connected a person is with the victim the more likely that person is to be the killer. At any rate, you can see how I arrived at my conclusion."

"I can see the logic of it, but logic can lead you astray."

"And there were a couple of other considerations. I needed at least three suspects rather than two. Two's not enough. It's kind of like a can of tennis balls."

"If you need another suspect to make it symmetrical why not just include yourself? Do you know your own blood type?"

"I do, as a matter of fact. It's type A. I'll be happy to include myself if you insist, but it's no fun since I can't take myself seriously as a suspect. Is it okay with you if we include Janice?"

"Fine. You're making the rules."

"You can appreciate now just how interesting our little disclosure scene is going to be." Durrell indicates the three index cards turned face down on the coffee table. Battles' envelope lies beside them. "We have here the blood types of Jack and Janice Abbott and Arthur Inman, and we have the report on the blood taken from the English Department." He reaches for the first card.

"Hold it just a second." Cory leans forward in the recliner. "Let me complicate your theory just a bit. Since we're reexamining all our assumptions, I'd like to reexamine one of yours if you don't mind."

"Feel free."

"Your assumption is that if the blood on the cleaning rag doesn't turn out to be Sanders', then it must be the killer's. That's a very shaky hypothesis."

"Let's make a distinction here." Durrell drops the card back on the table. "It's true that it can't be proven absolutely, but it's not a *shaky* hypothesis. It's very solid as hypotheses go. Let's say when we open the envelope we discover that the blood type is not AB. Okay? That means it's definitely not Sanders' blood. It means that Inman's story is almost certainly correct. It means that the blood was fresh on the following Friday night about 11:30. It means that somebody was in the locked English Office a week after the murder bleeding on the floor and failing to report the stench of a dead body in the next room. Who else but the killer?"

"And what exactly was the killer doing there a week after the murder and why was he bleeding?"

"Isn't it obvious?" Durrell's tone is one he might have used to address a not especially bright student. "He or she—we're using the masculine here but you understand we also have a female suspect—was bleeding because he cut himself on the sharp glass shards he went back to collect, presumably because the larger pieces and the wooden base had his fingerprints on them. And he may have removed other incriminating evidence."

"Such as?"

"It doesn't matter what. But there *is* evidence to support my theory. And doesn't it stand to reason that somebody in a highly nervous state trying to pick up all these pieces of glass and get the hell out of there could have nicked himself on the hand? That's all it would take—just a nick. You give *me* a better hypothesis to explain why there was fresh blood in a locked room a week after the murder."

"Assuming that it's not type AB."

"Right."

"I can't," Cory says. "It could have happened that way." Maybe they *are* going to find out who killed Sanders. "Go ahead with your demonstration."

"The moment of truth," Durrell says. "Here's the way we're going to do it. The three suspects are on the table. I will disclose their blood types in order of increasing suspicion—Inman, Janice, Jack. I'll also explain certain complications and implications as we go along."

"There are complications?"

"There could be but not if we're lucky." He reaches for the card on the left. "First is Inman." He flips it over to reveal a large

O printed with a red felt-tip pen. "As you see, type O, the most common type. If the blood in that lab report is type O, then we can posit several conclusions. It wasn't Sanders' blood and Inman's story is plausible. It was probably the killer's blood and Inman cannot be eliminated as a suspect, since he has the same type. Maybe he cut himself retrieving the glass and wiped up his own blood. Do you follow that?"

"I understand."

"I only hope it's not type O because there's a further complication." He flips the second card—another O. "You see, Janice is also type O, so if your envelope says type O we have a problem. We've proven that the rag doesn't contain Sanders' blood and we've verified Inman's story, but we haven't eliminated either Inman or Janice as suspects. We may have identified the killer as a person with type O blood, but that's forty-four percent of the population. Are you with me?"

"Yes. O would be complicated."

"Ah, but with Jack we have more interesting possibilities." He flips the last card—a scarlet B. "Jack, you see, is all alone at type B, so if your envelope says B, we have a very clean result—no complications. In that case we know that Inman is innocent and that Janice is innocent. At least of murder. We know that of our possible suspects only Jack could be guilty, and given everything else we know it pretty much seals it. I'm betting on B." He picks up the lab report and looks at it for a moment. "You have the honor of giving us the results."

He tosses it into Cory's lap, and Cory tears it across the end and blows into it, pulling out a single sheet of paper. When he reads it he feels confused at first, assuming that Durrell has anticipated every possibility.

"Am I right or not?" Durrell stands up from the sofa.

"You're half right," Cory says. "You're right that it's not Sanders' blood, which means that you may be right that we've got the killer's blood."

"Then why am I only half right? Is it type O? Dammit, I was

afraid of that."

"It's not type O. The blood on the rag was type A. I believe that's your type."

"Type A? Damn. The one thing I didn't want."

"None of your suspects have type A. It means that everybody's innocent."

"Not everybody." Durrell shakes his head and sits back on the sofa. "Damn."

*

Driving home later, Cory feels oddly depressed, and something he can't quite bring up into consciousness is nagging at him, a loose end, something he heard for a second and then let go. He should be feeling elated, he knows. Durrell has demonstrated that his friends are not murderers.

He draws a long breath and lets its out as he drives through the light at the Kingston Pike-Neyland Drive intersection, thinking, *We will never know who killed J. Hollis Sanders but it doesn't matter. It was nobody I know. Now I can let it go.* It's at that point, across from the Unitarian Church on Kingston Pike, that he becomes conscious of what's nagging at him. A slip of the tongue.

Four out of five ain't bad.

Something like that. And then forward to the next link. *Type A. Damn. The one thing I didn't want.*

An innocent slip of the tongue perhaps. Or did Durrell have *four* suspects, one that he was keeping to himself? Was there another index card in his philosophy text inscribed with a scarlet A?

SATURDAY

CHAPTER TWENTY-TWO
THE BLACK LEXUS

On Saturday afternoon Cory concludes, after some thought, that he's obliged to inform Owen Battles of the latest developments in the J. Hollis Sanders murder investigation. He hears the play-by-play of a baseball game on Battles' end as they talk about the lab report.

"Sorry to bother you at home, but I think this is important." What he suggests to Battles is that the blood on Inman's cleaning rag demonstrates that the custodian's story was true, that he was in all likelihood innocent of murder, and that there is a strong possibility that the murderer—a person with type A blood, a type possessed by about thirty-nine percent of the population—returned to the English Office a week after the murder to retrieve evidence and is still at large.

Battles, not surprisingly, is quite circumspect in his reply. He had of course looked at the report before passing it on, he tells Cory, and he had considered its implications. "Unofficially, I would say that there's a chance you're right. Officially, I would have to say that the investigation is closed."

"But shouldn't you at least give the information to the Chancellor? Why can't it be re-opened?" Cory, knowing that his effort is futile, feels it his duty to make it.

Battles responds that he had indeed called the Chancellor and given him the results of the blood test. "It got somewhat more complicated than I intended. I tried to leave the impression that the blood was submitted to the lab before the investigation was closed," Battles says. "But the Chancellor questioned me fairly closely on that, so I had to tell him about your call."

"It's okay. You simply told him the truth. And you told him the implications of the blood test on the cleaning rag?"

"Yes." Battles does not volunteer the Chancellor's response.

"Well, what did he say? Did he have anything to say?"

"My impression was that the investigation will not be re-opened. The Chancellor is satisfied that the findings of the investigation are substantially correct and we need to move on, as I believe he put it."

"But how does he explain the discrepancy of the blood types?"

Battles, selecting his words carefully, sounds stiff and unnatural in contrast to the television announcer in the background describing a catch against the wall in centerfield. "The Chancellor's view is that the blood was only a small part of a pattern of incriminating evidence against Inman."

"It was the most important piece of evidence. You know that."

"It's true that the blood on the cleaning rag led us to Inman in the first place, the Chancellor said, but now it appears that it had no connection to the crime. It could have been there for weeks, months. The great irony of this case, he said, is that the evidence that led to the arrest of the perpetrator turned out to be irrelevant."

"He's good. I'll have to give him that."

"The other evidence, he feels, is much stronger—the proximity, the criminal record, the fact that he disappeared after the murder was discovered. And he thinks that the suicide was proof that the conclusions of the investigation were justified."

"I see. What do *you* think?"

"I don't think anything officially. The Chancellor made it very clear that I should not go any further with it."

"If you *were* going to pursue it, what would you do?"

"Well, unofficially of course, I think I would try to track down a black Lexus, probably a 2012 model."

"When did *that* come up? I never saw any mention of it in the reports."

"It wasn't in the reports because it didn't mean anything until now." Battles is beginning to drop some of his reserve. "The security man in the dorm complex across the street from the Humanities Building told me on the Tuesday after the body was discovered that there was a black Lexus in the Humanities parking lot the night of the murder. He noticed it because it was the only car in the lot. It was the beginning of spring break and the students were gone. He didn't know when it left, but it was not there the next morning. He thinks it was also there briefly the following Friday night. He's not positive it was the same car, but it looked identical. Those were the only two times he's seen it there."

"Why didn't you mention it in the reports?"

"Because it was there *twice*, not just the night of the murder. There's a great deal of stuff that doesn't get in reports. That lot would be where a person would park if they were going to the Humanities Building."

"It doesn't seem like much."

"No, except that according to your theory the perpetrator was there twice, the two times that car was seen in the parking lot."

"I see your point. But you're not going to follow up on it?"

"No. But if I did, I'd check out everybody even remotely connected with Sanders to see what kind of car they drive."

"Anything else you would look at? If you were still interested in pursuing it, I mean."

"I think I would talk to a man named Charles Durrell. He's a professor in the English Department."

"Oh?"

"I had a phone call that suggested this fellow might be able to tell us something."

Silence on Cory's end.

"Are you still there?"

"You mean that this person might be implicated?"

"Either that or he might know something. I'd make a point to talk to him if I was still working on it."

"Anything else?" *Who made that phone call, Jack Abbott? Or is*

Durrell more deeply involved than he admits?

"Nothing I can think of."

"Do you mind if I check with you again sometime?"

"You can call me at home any time. I'm here after six and on the weekends. You understand that officially I have no connection with the case."

"I understand. But maybe you could give me a call if you remember something else. Do you have a pencil handy? I'd like to give you my home number."

"I wouldn't put too much hope in the car," Battles says after he takes down the number. "Statistically, only a small percentage of leads like that ever pan out."

Statistics can be very deceptive, Cory is thinking as he listens to the announcer in the background. "He's only hitting .250," the announcer is saying, "but that's no indication of his value to the Braves." He remembers a statistic he once read, so astonishing that he had doubted its validity until he worked it out. The difference between a .250 hitter, a marginal player, and a .300 hitter, a star, is one hit every twenty times at bat. One out of twenty. It goes against all reason, but there it is. The odds of tracking down a black Lexus should be better than one in twenty.

"You've been very helpful," Cory says.

"I'd appreciate it if you didn't mention this to the Chancellor. He wasn't too happy with me getting the ABO typing on the cleaning rag after the case had been officially closed."

"If I may ask, isn't it odd to have to report to a university chancellor?"

"It is a little odd," Battles says. "But he likes to keep up with anything potentially damaging to the university, so if you don't mind—"

"Not a word from me. I don't think I'll be talking to the Chancellor anyway. I don't think the Chancellor's going to want to see me for a while."

He sits silently at the desk for a few minutes after the call, trying to think it through. What keeps coming back is the way

Charles Durrell always seems to be in the middle of it. *What's he holding back?* He picks up the phone again and dials the number.

"What's on your mind?"

"Just killing time, Charles."

"I don't know what else there is to say. We pretty much reached the end of the road last night."

"You still working on your novel?"

"Not really. Maybe I'll get back to it at some point."

"I was wondering what you're going to do with it now that things have turned out like this. Now that all the prime suspects have been cleared, you need a new murderer. So who did it?"

"I haven't worked that out yet."

"Maybe the murderer drives a black Lexus."

Durrell does not respond immediately. "Why would you say something like that?"

"No reason. It just occurred to me."

"No, you seem to be making a point. Do you know something?"

"A black Lexus was seen in the Humanities parking lot on both Friday evenings. The only times it's been seen there. You can see the implication of that."

"It's a parking lot," Durrell says. "You'd expect to see cars parked there."

"Let me ask you the same question," Cory says. "Do you know something?"

"Nope."

"I got the impression last night that you knew something you weren't telling me—maybe something about a person with type A blood."

"I don't know where you got that idea," Durrell says. "It must have been your imagination."

"Must have been. But it's very strange, this sudden shift in mood. Last night you were flipping over index cards with blood types and today you don't want to talk about it."

"It's over. I was wrong. I had a theory about it but it turned out to be wrong."

"You know, given the title *Women in Cars* you might think of making the murderer a woman."

Another momentary silence. "Too obvious. Any seasoned mystery reader would jump to that conclusion right away."

He tries another tack. "What about this? Since the protagonist is a theorist, maybe the murderer ought to be somebody he hardly knows or maybe met just once or twice, say—not one of the major characters."

"What would be the point?"

"The point is that solving the mystery is purely theoretical. Has nothing to do with the real world."

"That would be cheating," Durrell says. "Readers would never sit still for that. It has to be somebody who figures prominently in the novel."

"Just an idea. If you don't like it, forget it."

"Are you trying to tell me something?"

"Nope. Just killing time."

"I'll have to think about that last idea," Durrell says. "Why doesn't the theorist get to know this character?"

"Perhaps because one of the other characters is protecting this, ah, person."

"A woman."

"Yes."

"What's her motive?"

"I have no idea about that. A man writing a novel should be able to could come up with a good motive. But on a related point, I was thinking we ought to celebrate the end of our little affair, such as it is. How about dinner tomorrow night? My treat—say Harry's at eight."

"I'm not sure I could make it tomorrow night," Durrell says.

He offers the bait. "Sally's going to be there." He hasn't mentioned it to her. "At least I'm assuming she will be. We've been sort of seeing each other lately, so I expect she'll be up to it. Actually, she thinks we ought to get back together on some basis, odd as that may seem—trying to pick up the pieces, as she put it."

He realizes that he wants Durrell's reaction, which does not come. "Is that stunned silence I hear? I thought you might be amused at the idea, given our history."

"*Amused* is not a word that comes to mind."

"What word does come to mind?"

"I'm not sure I could come up with one. I just hope you know what you're doing."

"I have no idea what I'm doing, but that's an odd thing to say. You're sure you don't know something I don't know?"

"Since I don't know what you know, that would be hard to say, but back to your invitation, I don't want to go through the Sanders thing any more. If that's what you're thinking, then count me out."

"We won't talk about it."

"This is the end, right? We're not going over it any more."

"Fine with me. No more talk about the great English Department mystery. I'll see you at eight."

But everything is changed by a follow-up conversation with Owen Battles in the late afternoon. He had phoned Battles to ask if there was by chance a license number for the black Lexus. "I'm afraid not," Battles tells him, "but I do have something else you might be interested in." His tone is understated, and Cory is not quite prepared for the sensational nature of the revelation that follows.

It appears that Inspector Roy Hutchins opened the trunk of his university car for some reason on Saturday afternoon and detected an odor. He located its source as an open plastic bag he had placed there some days earlier. It contained letters soiled with vomit he had collected from the out-tray on the secretary's desk in the English Office. He had thought nothing of them at the time, but his curiosity was aroused when he now saw that one of the stained envelopes, addressed to the university's chief counsel, had *Confidential* printed on it in large letters.

As Battles reads him the letter in his toneless official voice, Cory feels the hairs rise on the back of his neck as it begins to come together—the suspect Durrell would not reveal, the motive, the opportunity. "Let me get a pen. I need to make some notes. Do you mind starting again from the beginning?"

"*I need your legal advice on a somewhat delicate matter that has come to light in the department,*" Battles begins and reads down through Sanders' signature. "It doesn't prove anything, except maybe motive," he says, "but if you could fit it together with the blood type we just ran and the black Lexus, you might have something."

Afterwards, Cory looks over the notes he scribbled while Battles read and decides to drive over to the university bookstore, where he purchases a book called *The Rape of Literature* by Jennifer Reed.

SUNDAY

CHAPTER TWENTY-THREE
THE CHANCELLOR'S LOOSE ENDS

"Thanks for coming in on such short notice." The Chancellor, at his desk, looks up from a sheet of hand-written notes. "I hate to take you away from your week-end, but I need to tie up a couple of loose ends."

"No problem." James Houghton, dressed in jeans and a black polo, closes the door behind him. "Are we talking about Sanders?"

"It won't go away."

"There's a lot of speculation out there." Houghton takes a chair in front of the desk.

"That's our first problem. What are they saying?"

"About what you'd expect. That the janitor didn't do it. That the investigation was closed prematurely. That it was a crime of passion. That the murderer is still out there. Along those lines."

"And do they name names?"

"There are some names being bandied about—Jack Abbott, Charles Durrell, Jennifer Reed. Apparently, Abbott and Sanders were engaged in a shouting match just before spring break, and Abbott has been acting odd lately. Of course the animosity between Sanders and the other two is of long standing."

"Let me stop you right there for a minute. Professor Reed is one of my loose ends." The Chancellor consults his notes.

"When did she come into the picture."

"I got a phone call from Battles. It seems the investigation belatedly turned up a letter written by Sanders in which Professor Reed figures prominently. Do some of your rumors have to do with her sexual orientation?"

"Jennifer Reed's never tried to hide her sexual orientation. She's been consistently a vocal supporter of gay rights, same-sex marriage, issues like that."

"I'm aware of that. I was referring to her personal, ah, proclivities."

"Michael, this is the twenty-first century. Her personal sex life, whatever her proclivities, is not an issue in the university."

"This is a little more complicated than her personal sex life." The Chancellor hesitates, as if about to pursue the argument further, then backs off. "It could certainly be an issue with certain citizens of our fair state, but let's drop Professor Reed."

Houghton, curious now, gestures toward the Chancellor's notes. "You want to tell me about it?"

O'Connor shakes his head. "I don't think I do. I think I'm going to let this sleeping dog lie." He folds the sheet of notes, pushes it aside, and opens a slim folder. "Any other names being bandied about?"

"It's just talk, Michael. I wouldn't worry about it too much."

"I'm inclined to agree with you," O'Connor says. "Let people talk. These are academics. They talk but they don't actually *do* anything, so nothing's going to come of that. On the other hand, I've got another little problem that might lead to something unpleasant." He gestures toward the open folder. "And I'm afraid it's of my own making."

"Anything I can do to help?"

"I just need a sounding board," O'Connor says. "I hate to admit it, but Edgar was right. Robert Cory turned out to be a mistake. Actually, a huge mistake."

"How's that?"

"He won't let it go. He's convinced that a wrong has been done, and he's trying to set it right. He was the one responsible for running the blood test on the cleaning rag on the day *after* I had relieved him of his duties."

"I didn't know about that. What was the result?"

"Never mind about that now," O'Connor says. "That's another issue. Right now the problem is what to do about Cory."

"Why not confront him?"

"Well, you see the trouble is I don't have any authority over him. That was my mistake—getting somebody from outside the system."

"Then just a gentle reminder of the harm he could do?"

"Perhaps," O'Connor says. "My reading of him is that he thinks of himself as a person of integrity. I just don't want to get his back up. If it becomes a matter of principle, he may decide, say, to take it to the newspapers, and then we're in double jeopardy—a re-opened murder investigation and a cover-up."

"How do you know all this—I mean that he's still pursuing it?"

"Battles. Cory's been in touch with him. Told him he thinks Inman's innocent. Appears to be tracking down leads—the amateur detective."

"Do you think he knows something?"

"I have no idea, but you see my dilemma," O'Connor says. "There's a man out there trying to re-open the case, pursuing his own investigation, but any pressure I put on him is apt to make things worse, blow the whole thing up."

"So do nothing and hope for the best, that he doesn't uncover anything unpleasant."

"The best outcome would be that there's nothing for him to uncover." The Chancellor closes the folder. "Thanks for your input. I think I agree with you on that—don't push it. But we may have to come back to Jennifer Reed at some point."

Houghton notes that the folder is labeled simply *Cory*. "Cory knows several of the people involved, right?"

"That's right."

"So maybe whatever it is he uncovers would be as unpleasant for him as it would be for us."

CHAPTER TWENTY-FOUR
THE UNRAVELING AT HARRY'S

Despite its unassuming name, Harry's is widely regarded as the best restaurant in town, certainly the most expensive, the reservation of choice for anniversaries and birthdays. It boasts an imported Tuscan chef and an extensive wine list, but the feature generally credited for its success is architectural. From the art deco foyer one enters the bar and dining room by descending a sweeping flight of gently-graded stairs that could have come from a forties musical. Harry correctly surmised that one reason to patronize a restaurant as expensive as his own was to be seen, and his enormous staircase assures that every entrance is an occasion.

On Sunday evening Cory sits at Harry's bar and watches his ex-wife at the top of the stairs scanning the room. When she spots him, she smiles and descends in a black dress that looks to have been fashioned expressly for walking down stairs. Her manner announces her indifference to the roomful of eyes that follow her down, but the lone man sitting two stools down from Cory offers the room's judgment. "Jesus," he mutters under his breath.

"Nice dress," Cory says as she approaches. He's pretty sure he recognizes it.

"It's Cynthia's. She insisted I wear it, said it was perfect for Harry's."

"You told her?"

"She was very jealous. She still hasn't said a word about dropping in on you the other night, and I'm pretending I don't know. She thinks it's her little secret but now it's mine."

"She's right about the dress." *So we all have our little secrets—or think we do.* The dress, he sees, is the one that Cynthia had insisted was properly worn only without undergarments. One secret exposed.

"You never took me to places like this when we were married," she says.

"We were poor, remember? Do you want a drink? Our table's ready."

"A drink would be lovely." She motions to the bartender. "Perhaps I'll have one of those pink things they drank on *Sex and the City*," she says, as if innocent of the names of alcoholic beverages.

"A cosmopolitan," the bartender says.

"That's it. Could you have it sent to the table?"

The host seats them next to a very young couple who are studying the menu in silence.

"I don't know if Charles is coming," Cory says. "He was a little reluctant."

"He'll be here," she says. "Remind me what it is exactly we're doing."

"You were just saying we ought to see each other more, so here we are for a nice dinner."

"But this is a nice dinner for three. Why Charles?"

"Let's just say we're celebrating the end of a brief episode, whatever it was that started on Monday, and here we are at the end on Sunday—a very interesting week. Here's Charles."

Durrell stands at the top of the stairs, surveying the room below. He is wearing his customary corduroy jacket and blue work shirt, but has added a tie. "Maybe we should have gotten Cynthia to dress him," Cory says.

He walks down the stairs, and in the silence they hear the commentary of the couple at the next table as they peruse the wine list. They settle on iced tea, much to the distress of the young woman, who protests, "But it's our *anniversary*," then looks over to see if she has been overheard.

Charles Durrell does not appear happy to be at Harry's. "Christ, this place is unbelievable."

"I think you two know each other." Cory waves him to the empty chair.

"Hello, Sally." He leans down to kiss the top of her head, his hand on her shoulder. *Like old friends*, Cory is thinking. "So this is where the rich people eat." He slouches in his chair and takes in the dining room.

"You've never been here? The city's most fabled restaurant?" Cory hands him the wine list.

"It's a point of honor which I've now compromised thanks to you two."

"Don't blame me," Sally says. "Robert picked it."

"Don't worry, I'm buying."

"I should hope so. Look at these prices." Durrell scans the wine list.

"Harry's still paying off the staircase," Cory says. "I was thinking of ordering the Brunello." He catches the waiter's eye. "Is that okay?"

Durrell locates it on the list. "Fine. If paying that much for a bottle of wine makes you feel important, go ahead."

"We'll have the outrageously expensive Brunello di Montalcino," he says to the waiter. "And send a bottle to the couple at the next table."

"Any message?"

"Just say happy anniversary from Harry's."

"My goodness. What's got into you?" Sally looks up at him with a trace of a smile.

"I feel like celebrating."

The word catches Durrell's attention. "Celebrating *what*?"

"The solution to the mystery."

Durrell stands up and pushes his chair back with a clatter that interrupts the muted ambiance of Harry's. "I thought I made it clear. I came because you swore it was over."

"Something interesting came up after I talked to you."

192

"I don't care what came up, I'm out."

"Charles. This is so uncharacteristic of you. I mean, just days ago you were orchestrating the whole thing. We were comparing blood types on three-by-five cards. What the hell's going on?"

"It's over."

"Doesn't that tell you something?" Cory turns to Sally. "As long as it was a game he loved it, but now it's not a game. He knows something and he's not sharing it. What could that possibly be?"

She looks up at Durrell. "It's okay, Charles. Sit down."

It's okay? What is it between them? "Please sit down," Cory says softly. The young couple at the next table are looking over. "I indulged you for days. You owe me fifteen minutes at least. I'll lay it out very simply, and you can tell me yes or no. And that'll be the end of it."

"We're already at the end."

"Fifteen minutes."

Durrell sits down and the couple at the next table turn their attention to the waiter bringing a bottle of wine.

Durrell assumes a bored expression and looks out across the dining room. "I don't think you want to do this. You don't know what you're doing."

"That sounds almost like an anonymous note I once received. You didn't write that note, did you Charles?"

"You know as well as I do that Jack Abbott wrote that note. But it was something of a red herring, wasn't it? He wrote it because he was afraid of what you might discover about his wife. But he was wrong, and it led nowhere."

"That was my conclusion also," Cory says. "It was a distraction. Here's the wine."

"Your Brunello, sir." They sit in silence as the waiter makes an elaborate display of decanting and pouring the wine. "Would anyone care for an appetizer?"

"Maybe later. Give us about fifteen minutes if you don't mind," Cory says. "We're in the middle of something." He pauses until the waiter is out of range. "We're in agreement on the note then. Let's take it a step further."

"Just remember that what you're doing has consequences," Durrell says.

"I recall that was something I was saying to you a couple of days ago. We seem to have switched sides."

"Why don't you just tell us what you found," Sally says.

"Is this pure speculation on your part?" Durrell leans forward, frowning.

"Mostly fact," Cory says. "A letter actually, although there is one assumption."

"And that would be?"

"That would be your reluctance to reveal your own suspicions. In particular, your suspicion of one of your colleagues, a feminist whose hatred for the department head exceeds even your own."

"So that's where you're heading." Durrell's expression is not what Cory expected, sitting back in his chair with a trace of a smile. "Okay, let's see what you've got."

"Let's say you've had a sort of wild surmise about this woman all along, but you're afraid to admit it to yourself. You're fond of her." Cory holds up his hand when Durrell threatens to interrupt. "So you seize on the associate head and lead us in that direction— off the scent, so to speak. You even come to believe that it *is* the associate head when events begin to fall into place—the note, the crazy behavior, the rumored affair. Then, there's the crucial scene with the blood types and the theory falls apart."

He's interrupted by a commotion in the dining room, a scattering of applause and boos.

"Our beloved mayor," Sally says, and Cory looks up to see a short plump man accompanied by a younger woman descend the stairs. He's smiling broadly and performing a parody of a campaign wave.

"Where was I?"

"The blood types," Durrell says.

"Yes. The blood types. Let's say that you actually have the blood types of *four* people, not just the three you produce. I distinctly remember 'four out of five ain't bad.'" He interprets Durrell's uneasiness as a concession. "And let's say that the blood type on the cleaning rag turns out to be type A, which absolves the three obvious suspects but matches the fourth. The odds are turning against her, but you resolve to keep this discovery to yourself. You see the irony here. You actually *have* solved the mystery—your blood theory was right—but you can't take credit for your brilliant solution to the murder. You can't reveal the results, since it would put your friend under suspicion."

He senses that Durrell, who sips his wine without much interest, is becoming increasingly uncomfortable. "Jennifer," he says. "What's her motive?"

"That's fairly complicated. The whole solution turns on the fact that a letter written by the department head on the day he was killed gets misplaced for almost a week."

"Already your scenario's in trouble," Durrell says.

"No, there's a perfectly logical reason for it that I need not go into at the moment. Those things happen. Sloppy police work essentially. Anyway, when this letter comes to light after the investigation is closed, it reveals that the department head is threatening to expose this woman as a way of getting her out of the department. He has information that could wreck her career."

"So he finally found something."

"Did you know about this?"

"No, but it's the only part of your story that rings true."

Cory reaches inside his jacket. "Just let me finish, then you can tell me where I'm wrong." He pulls out several folded sheets. "These are my notes from a conversation yesterday with Owen Battles of the campus police. He read me the letter, and its implications don't require much interpretation. This is not a transcription, and I may have missed some things but I got the gist of it."

"Go ahead. Let's get it all out."

"It's dated the day of the murder, printed out on the department head's personal stationary, and I'm guessing on his own printer, which would explain why his secretary never saw it.

It's addressed to the university counsel, a woman named Jessica Champion. And it says in effect that he needs her legal advice on a somewhat delicate matter. He talked that afternoon to a faculty member, and he names her—Jennifer Reed—and confronted her with information sufficient in his judgment to force her dismissal. She denied the accusation, but he was able to give her the name of one of the students involved—the fact that there are students involved would be the principal grounds for her dismissal. She did not deny knowing the student, and he led her to understand he had other names."

"These are male students or female students?" Sally asks.

"Female. That's made clear later on. To continue. He let Professor Reed know that he was the only administrator aware of her indiscretion, and told her that if she agreed to certain conditions her story would end with him. If she resigned quietly, he would not reveal any information and would assist her in securing a position elsewhere. If she refused to leave quietly, she would be fired, and if she contested her dismissal he was prepared to reveal all the sordid details. He referred her to a passage in the Faculty Handbook that would be the basis for her dismissal. He told her not only would her dismissal be upheld on the grounds of moral turpitude by any faculty committee in the country, but she could never teach again for any responsible university. Then he asks the counsel for legal advice on several possible courses of action."

"Is that all?" Sally asks.

"It goes on, but you get the flavor of it. It appears that she was involved with an undergraduate intern who worked in something called Computer Assisted Registration."

"CARS. It's called CARS," Durrell says. "It's a division of the registrar's office."

"Well, this woman in CARS—"

"This gets more outrageous the longer it goes on."

"The letter exists. I might even be able to get it for you, although I'm told that the smell is pretty bad—your head secretary threw up on it. Anyway, this woman in CARS apparently met Sanders at some affair and said enough to get him suspicious. Lover's quarrel maybe, a woman scorned. I don't know what exactly, but he sniffed it out, and of course he had his own motives for wanting to uncover something on Professor Reed sufficient to get her out of his department. And these days you apparently can't get away with having sex with students even if you're a woman."

Durrell looks out across the dining room. "So he finally got her."

"Or vice versa. But what do you think? Does it sound at all plausible?"

"Maybe in a novel," Durrell says. "Not in this case. It doesn't sound plausible that she would just walk into his office and kill him."

"I agree," Cory says. "But that's not what happened. All the evidence indicates that it was not premeditated. She returns to his office, let's say, to try to reason with him. There's a violent confrontation taken one step too far. Imagine Sanders and Jennifer Reed alone in his office on Friday evening. They argue. Maybe he even tried to make a play for her, her sexual preference notwithstanding . And if he did, it's the one act that permits a woman to take a life, or so she believes."

"How could you possibly know that?"

"I read her book last night."

He stops to catch their reaction. "Self-defense then," Sally says. "Not murder."

"Perhaps," Cory says, "but we would only have her word on that."

"It's interesting," Durrell says, "but it *is* pure speculation. You hardly know the woman."

"I read her book."

"And there's no real evidence against her."

"The letter in itself doesn't prove anything except motive, as Owen Battles said yesterday. But he said if I could put it together with the blood type and a black Lexus, I would have something. I'm betting that you know Jennifer's blood type and I'm betting that she drives a black Lexus."

Sally looks at him, frowning now. "When did the car come into it?"

"It was parked in a lot nearby on the night of the murder *and* the night that the killer apparently returned to retrieve the broken glass with fingerprints and whatever else had been left in Sanders' office. And of course in the process left fresh blood in the carpet. At least that was your theory." He smiles at Durrell. "So it's a simple question. Does Jennifer drive a black Lexus?"

"Jennifer drives a Honda," Durrell says.

He hadn't counted on that. "The car's not crucial to the solution," he says finally. "A match would have been nice but it's not crucial. There's still the blood type."

"Is that all?"

"It's enough. Two out of three. I'd be satisfied with that."

"Nothing else?"

"That's it."

"That's what you brought us to this absurd place to hear?"

"Come on, Charles. Admit that you suspected her from the beginning."

"The problem with your little solution is quite fundamental," Durrell says. "If it were a legal brief I believe the term would be 'fatally flawed.' The simple truth is that Jennifer Reed didn't kill Sanders, and I never suspected that she did."

"I think you're letting your feelings get the better of your judgment," Cory says.

Durrell's laugh is sardonic. "God, this is crazy. How can I stop it?"

"Are you denying that you had a female suspect from the beginning?"

"I'm not denying anything, but I don't have to justify myself to you."

"Are you denying that you checked on a fourth person's blood type without revealing it to me?"

Durrell's voice is very quiet. "I never checked Jennifer's blood type."

"I'm not sure you're telling me the whole truth."

Durrell shakes his head. "So far as I know Jennifer doesn't have type A blood. Of course you could always check that out. I could have my friend work on it."

"What about the *fifth* name, the one your friend couldn't find. Was that Jennifer's name?"

"No."

'Then whose name was it? Do you mind telling me?"

"It was your name."

"You're lying. You're trying to protect her. Why would you possibly suspect *me*?"

"Do you have any evidence at all?"

"Just what I've told you. Perhaps you know somebody else who drives a black Lexus and has type A blood."

"What if it was just a horrible accident?" Sally says in a quiet voice.

"I can't take any more of this," Durrell drains his glass of wine. "I'll pass on dinner. I've got some things I need to do." He stands up from the table and drops his napkin in the chair. "Goodbye, Sally." He leans down to her and they embrace awkwardly in silence.

She knows what he knows. Cory watches from his chair, knowing that he's crossed some boundary. *What is it that they share*? "Please stay, Charles. I'll drop it. That's it, no more loose talk. It's over." But Durrell is already striding away, and they watch him as he walks across the dining room and up the wide staircase.

"Why would he just walk away like that? Doesn't that tell you he's holding something back? He knows something." Cory pauses. "And maybe you know what it is."

"He knows I drive a black Lexus."

Cory pours himself another glass of Brunello di Montalcino. A drop runs down the stem onto the white tablecloth. "I guess a lot of people drive a car like that. I didn't—"

"And he knows that Hollis and I had been seeing each other."

"Why are you telling me this?"

She leans close to him across the small table, and places her hand on his arm. Her voice is almost a whisper, and an observer might have seen them as lovers sharing an intimate secret. "I want you to stop. You would have put it together eventually. You're not as quick as Charles, but you're more dogged, and that's why I need you to stop. I need you to stop asking questions. Please. I need you to stop talking to that policeman. You're putting me in jeopardy and it's not what you think."

"What do I think?"

"You think it was a murder. It wasn't. It was just a horrible accident. If his head hadn't hit the table I don't think—I don't know. All I know for sure is I was trying to protect myself."

He takes a sip of wine without finding anything to say.

"Can't you understand? I was trying to protect myself."

"If it was self-defense why wouldn't you go to the police?"

"You are so naive. *I* know it was self-defense, but what would other people think? I could be sent to prison just for trying to defend myself. I'm not guilty of anything. It was like a car wreck, and I was able to walk away from it—until you stirred it all up again. Why can't you just let it alone?" She holds his eyes for a long time then leans back slowly and looks away.

He feels the constriction in his chest. "You think I'll protect you, don't you?"

"You're an honorable man. You'll think about it for a very long time. And then you'll decide that if I'm telling the truth it would be more of an injustice to put me at risk." She leans toward him once more. "And I am telling the truth. You can see that, can't you?"

"I don't know. I'll have to think about it." He stands up, fishes his wallet out of his jacket and throws some bills on the table. "Are you ready to leave?"

"Yes," she says. "We ought to go."

They walk in silence across the dining room and up the stairs. Outside, he finds a newspaper rack and picks up a copy of the Sunday *Journal*. "Did you park in the lot?"

"It's the black one over there."

He doesn't need to look. He looks down instead at a headline on the front page—*University's First Murder Case Officially Closed.* "You're right. I'm not very quick."

She takes his arm. "Charles had the advantage. He knew that Hollis and I had embarked on this stormy little affair, and he knew I was trying to break it off. That's why I was the fourth name on his list and you were the fifth—your Jack to my Janice."

"How does he know so much about you?"

"We're friends. We talk."

He nods. "I didn't know you were close." What were the odds? Before the event, astronomical. Afterwards, one in one. They walk across the parking lot toward the black Lexus, and she grips his arm.

"There's a great deal I could tell you," she says. "The one thing you have to understand is that there was no murder."

"What was it then?"

"A murder is something that takes place in detective novels and newspapers. This is something that just happened—like being attacked in an alley."

They are at her car now, and she leans against the door, looking up at him. "It wasn't a murder, and I'm not a murderer. I want you to understand that. I was defending myself. There was this glass thing on the desk—"

"Please. Not now."

"You don't know what it's like to have a secret so horrible, and you can't tell anybody."

"You *wanted* me to know," he says. "It's not just that you want me to stop asking questions. You want to implicate me. You want me to have to bear the burden of it."

"Maybe," she says. "You're the one that threw me to the wolves. We could have worked it out, maybe even now, but you just walked away."

"You want me to tell you it's all right—what you did. That he was an evil person and that you had no choice."

"He was attacking me. What choice did I have?"

"We ought to go," he says.

"What choice did I have?"

He looks at her without knowing how to reply. "Now *I* have to live with it," he says finally. "That's what you want, isn't it? I don't know that I've done anything to deserve that."

"Then you know how it feels," she says.

He watches her drive out of the lot and on to Kingston Pike, then walks back to the BMW, throws the newspaper in the back seat and drives home.

Later, in the study, he sits sipping a whiskey and looking at the far wall, the newspaper scattered on the floor beside the chair. The silence is broken by the telephone and he carries his whiskey over to the desk and punches it on.

"Please don't hang up."

He can hear traffic noise in the background. "Where are you?"

"In the driveway," she says. "I'm coming in. I'm going to tell you everything from the beginning and you can decide what you have to do."

"No need for that," he says. "There's no decision. I've got no choice."

"I'm coming in," she says.

"Sally, it's over."

"Even so."

He holds the phone to his ear until the line goes dead, then carries his whiskey back to the recliner, leans down and shuffles through the newspaper until he locates the box scores. Half aware of the click of heels in the entrance hall, he sees that on Saturday the Cardinals lost to the Reds, who rallied with two runs in the bottom of the ninth.

B. J. Leggett is Professor Emeritus of The University of Tennessee, Knoxville, where he held the title of Distinguished Professor of Humanities. He is the author of numerous studies of modern poetry and criticism, including books on A. E. Housman, Philip Larkin, and Wallace Stevens. *Women in Cars* is his third novel. The previous two, *Prosperity* and *Playing Out the String*, were published by Livingston Press.